Nellie's Devils
and other stories

Michael Glover

Nellie's Devils
and other stories

Michael Glover

1889 books

Nellie's Devils and other stories
Copyright © Michael Glover 2022
The moral rights of the author have been asserted.

Cover image © Albert @OwdAlbert 2021
Many thanks for this permission Albert – you're a gent!
Photographic montage of author on the back cover
courtesy Joseph Dupré

Morrison's Trousers, Nellie's Devils and Anna's Purse
were first broadcast on BBC Radio 3 and 4

www.1889books.co.uk
ISBN: 978-1-915045-05-8

For Ruth,
my forever evergreen

CONTENTS

The Letters	1
Morrison's Trousers	9
Nellie's Devils	17
The Rabbit and the Hare: a Crisis of Identity	26
Hand in Hand	28
Love. Love. Love	33
The Puzzle	35
Anna's Purse	37
Custard	51
Big, Bad Laughter	53
A Day to Remember	55
Detachment	66
Losing Him	76
The Bechstein Room	78
Revolutions	84

THE LETTERS

Puccini visited once! Henry James even mentioned it in a letter, I believe. Did I ever tell you that? We'd got to the house so late – the last sleeper from Rome. Sleep! That was always a joke. There was always too much to see, too much to be alive to. What lives they all lived!

Then there was a flood in the basement. They told us that the moment we arrived, so weary, with our baggage. They were standing outside in the courtyard, in front of the house – I remember it as though it were yesterday – looking so distressed, a little ring of them, encircling my great-aunt on my father's side, the matriarch, as we always used to call her.

Not distressed on *their* behalf though. On ours. We were their guests. We had come from so far. Ireland. The ancestral homeland. What a woman she was though, my great-aunt, formidable as any Apennine peak! And that laugh of hers! We got swept up into her. It was like being sucked into a great tornado – think of Dante's representation of Paolo and Francesca. Think of all the sadness of their thwarted love. Just think of it. I do, often.

Goodness knows how many years ago that was. What I remember most of all is her generosity, how they brought tins of fagioli, fresh pasta, everything we could possibly have needed. It's all in the latest box of letters. I was reading about it yesterday morning..

Some mornings I wake up before him, and slip across to the desk at the other end of the house. We sleep up there because of the views of the sea. It's such a lovely house to live in, ours, almost on the shingle.

That's where I tend to keep them, beside my mother's

old teak desk, at a slight angle to the window, with the telescope at my back. We're such stargazers. That's my place of work too. It's where I do all my reading, and all my careful transcribing. They are all gathered in heaps at my feet, silted up you could say, if you chose to be unkind to me, as he so often is. It's just as if the sea has pushed them there, over days, weeks. Some little bundles are tied together, oh so carefully, in red ribbon, perishable red ribbon, as if they were legal documents. I don't need to read much for it all to come alive to me again. David says I'm obsessed, but I know I'm not. Absorption, a profound absorption, a profound, life-long preoccupation, is never an obsession. I need it, I tell him. I need to define myself against it. I am the outcome of all those letters.

Whenever I slip into Westminster Cathedral, I always naturally cleave to the right, and then sit down in front of the mosaic of Istanbul, because of the family connections. I can spend hours just staring at that image. I find it so soothing, so enriching, forever outwardly expanding. It's what I tend to do when we go back to London, which always seems so far away these days. We go back so seldom. Perhaps we should let the place go. Except that we don't. We couldn't, could we? There would be too much to lose of everything that we once were, wouldn't there?

We have our daily routines, David and I. Nothing starts too early. We get up. He does his fifteen minutes in the sea. Such ferocious chopping through the waves! Too cold for me. It's good for him though. He does so love it. I just lie back in bed up here and think, think, watching the clouds hurrying past the skylight, about their usual cloud-business. I slip out into the morning cold, and then rush back to bed with a little bundle. I like fingering them. Old things have always had such an appeal to me, being an archaeologist. How can anyone bear to throw anything away? It would be like throwing away oneself. I just do not understand how people could let it happen.

After he's back, we have our coffee, slowly. Everything begins fairly slowly. Why hurry? What's the point of it? We both spent a lifetime of hurrying. Once upon a time. Then I tell him about what I've been reading. He usually comments. But then, after a minute or two, he falls asleep, like a baby. His head lolls against the chair back. I put a cushion under it – to make him comfortable. It's so tiring, pitting yourself against the sea, I think as I look at his lips, gently puffing out. Even when it's a slack tide. I do have to keep him in line. Only swim when it's a slack tide, I always tell him. I don't want you disappearing altogether.

They always took their holidays on Achill Island, my family. They were twitchers, all of them, even Agatha, for all her stoutness, and in the worst of weather. And there was always such weather on Achill! It would descend on you from nowhere, like a clap of thunder. Those monstrous clouds would roll in, and that would be it, for the day. Nothing would stop her though. She would flap her great arms about on the upstairs landing, shrieking out orders, getting them busy with all the preparations. What a tornado that woman was! She could boss people around like nobody's business. I have her binoculars, no one else wanted them. Can you believe that? That no one would want a pair of antique binoculars, in their old cracked leather case? I imagine her looking through them, getting ever more breathless because she was so asthmatic. Goodness knows how they carried her through the dunes, given the general state of her health. She did so love to eat though. Food was such a comfort to her. That was the other great challenge, of course, carrying the food for the picnic! One or two extras would have to be brought in for the day, from the village. That was no problem though. There were always young girls at a loose end, mooning their lives away, eager to grasp at the odd penny, the poor little mites, thin as straws they were...

What I have never really understood is how Patrick

came to be her brother. Don't get me wrong though. He really *was* her brother. But they were so different, he so lean and quiet and philosophical... He couldn't wait to become a seminarian. Was he sixteen when he left for good, with his trunk? Grandmother's old trunk, still with its peeling stickers. Surely not that young! I have no doubts that he called out to God long before God called out to him. He was so keen to get away, to answer the call.

I love Patrick, even though I only knew him as a very old man. I love everything that he represented, his sense of duty, his faith, his writings. He wrote so much! His trunk is full of his letters. No space for anything else. That will be my next year's task, to read his letters too, after I have done with hers. I love the idea of having a complete picture, of getting to the bottom of the beloved man. And I do still love him, with a passion.

I love his faith. Well, perhaps I love the *idea* of his faith, the faith of a man such as himself, enduring decade after decade, living in that cold monastery with nothing to do except contemplate the mysteries of his God. The low mutterings of prayer as the light fell, until the chapel was in complete darkness, with the exception of a single guttering candle. I could imagine doing it myself. Were I a believer, which I am not, I could have done it. I have his prayer books, his catechisms, his manuals of soulfulness as I always call them, all those books of his, and all so well thumbed, the leather so pummelled and punished by long and loving use and re-use, daily, even hourly.

I have spent days with my magnifying glass, trying to decipher his handwriting, that beautiful hand of his, always so cryptic and so private seeming, the black ink that he used, the very thin sideways strokes of his pen, always so thin and so well considered. By the time that I knew him well, he was a husk of himself, a tiny, shrunken thing, almost lost inside his cassock, which he always insisted on wearing. It defined him, you see. It held body and soul together. It knitted the two together, you could even say. I used to feel so sad when I visited him, in that home for retired religious. They all looked so shrunken and so lonely, every last one of them. Well, they would be though, wouldn't they? They had spent their entire lives being together and yet not together, huddled, the many as one, in a single room, and yet each one always alone with his God. Fundamentally alone, that's how it was, to be accountable only to invisible powers that were not of this earth, that's how they were. That was the living source of their profound contentment, their profound set-apartness. The nunnery was a mile or more away, on higher ground. I never visited, needless to say, though I did see them from time to time, in the town, doing their chores for one and all, those heaped wicker baskets of theirs. Once, a young one stumbled and fell, and out came the turnips, rolling down the road, a good dozen of them or more. We all went running after. Luckily, the poor girl was not too badly bruised. Her hair popped out when she fell. It was a lovely light blonde in hue, so unusual. I think that's what embarrassed her most of all, how in falling her hair had shaken loose, how she had shown to the world her lovely head of hair.

They kept them apart in the home too, male and female, always, which I also felt was a little sad. But it was necessary, they told me that, that compassionate couple who ran the place, who had founded it goodness knows when. It would be too much of a risk to do otherwise. A life of discipline can be a dangerous thing, they told me. They always spoke very quietly, as if reading, very slowly, and very attentively, from a sacred text. I nodded. I understood. My head found itself bowed too, when I sat in front of them, in their pokey little office with its grubby yellow skylight, almost as if by instinct. One time a nun had lifted up her skirt and smiled, beatifically. That sort of thing had gone on – and sometimes worse – in the mixing days. They'd quickly learnt to do things differently. They just couldn't risk it. They couldn't risk the closure of such a valuable community resource.

I don't know what else I do with the day, not really. It just goes when I get lost in the letters. David thinks that I read too much, that I should be doing more, in the garden, for example, taking more vigorous exercise, for example. I've never been one for exercise for its own sake though. I'm fit enough. Young looking too for my age, David tells me when he kisses me. That happens when he first wakes up. It's the first thing he does after he opens his eyes. And if I'm not there, if I'm already at my desk over in the far corner, just beyond his sightline, he calls out, wailing like a man lost at sea. Kiss! A kiss! Just the one word. And then I climb over the boxes, and give him my cheek. That's the way it is between us. I smile when I do it, of course. My little call of duty, that's how I always think of it. It's quite lovely in its way.

I remember now that she showed me the visitors' book when we first arrived, on that evening of the flood. It had a yellow silk head band, keeping it open at the page. She pointed down to it with such pride, such tears of joy in her eyes. *The* Puccini? I said, looking up at her. There is only one Puccini, she replied, quite quietly, quite modestly, looking down too and smiling faintly, almost as if she too might have seen him. I was so pleased for her that I half-believed that she *did* – for her sake. I so much wanted to humour her, and of course to take pride in the fact that I too, in some way that was not entirely clear to myself, had greeted him, because I was of the same Irish family. I too, had I been there, would have welcomed him, with open arms, the great Puccini, that dear little man!

'Do you remember about Puccini, darling?' I said to him over our coffees, as I waited for mine to cool a little. He often came very close to burning the milk. We were both sitting on the high stools in the kitchen, as we always did when we ate our morning porridge. He gave me a little smirk. 'That tiny scrawl in your great-aunt's visitor's book? Is that what you mean? I hope she read it right!' I felt so angered and disgusted by him that I got up and went upstairs.

He joined me later, when I was already deep into my reading. He likes to sit nearby when I am working so that he can fall asleep over his book with me nearby. I like it too. I do like to hear him breathing. One thing he has never been is a snorer.

Aunt Agatha had been describing the complicated arrangements for the arrival of the bishop, how someone would have to wait at the end of the lane, and yet another at the entrance gate, for however long it might take, because the dear man was so unreliable, and the house itself so inaccessible. *The price that one chooses to pay for a location of truly outstanding natural beauty* is all that my grandfather would offer by way of a response when they complained. And then there would be someone else primed to run out from the porch with the grey umbrella, the special one, more than large enough to encompass the vestments of a bishop. No one liked the bishop. No one liked his horrible, haughty English voice, and the way that he held forth at the table as if everything he said must be right because his was the resounding voice of the bishop, wasn't it? We girls laughed at his name too: Percy. *Bitty Little Percy* we would call him behind his back. Be careful that *Bitty Little Percy* doesn't get water down his neck between the car door and the house. Be sure to hold the umbrella at the right angle because we would never hear the last of it, would we, if the sacred neck just happened to get wet as a result of some Irish child's carelessness?

How we laughed! What are you laughing at? David said. I must have woken him. I blushed. I smiled. 'Bitty Little...'. 'Percy,' he added, wearisomely closing his eyes again. I let my anger settle, and then I went on reading. I imagined us all around that dining table again, with Patrick gone. He had gone so early, long before I was born. I wanted to think about him sitting around that table, talking in that quiet way of his. But when I tried to imagine him there, as a clever, restless boy of a young man, sitting there at the table, with a book open on his lap, half there and half lost in his thoughts, I found it was the old man who was facing me, the one I had known so briefly in the home, half-propped up in his bed, pillows well plumped up so that we could face each other.

I used to take a book out – he had his own little shelf – one of the ones they had brought to the home, a choice selection from his library, because they thought that the sight of his books, even the very few that the limited space would allow, would give him comfort. And so I took one out. Kierkegaard. *Either/Or* by Soren Kierkegaard. I said his name, very clearly, syllable by syllable, because by then he was profoundly deaf. I opened it at a random page and looked at all his tiny black scribblings. They practically engulfed the text. There were always so many questions! He took the book from me, and raised it to his cheek, rubbing it up and down, as if he were shaving himself.

I felt such a tenderness towards him then. He was smiling, but it was more an inward than an outward smile, as if he were communicating not so much with me as with his ideas, which were perhaps coming alive again within him. I like to think that that's how it was. Perhaps I am right. The next thing that happened was a sudden snatch of bird song, just beyond the window sill. I could see that in some way Patrick had registered it because he cocked his head to one side, and then made a sound, as if in imitation. *Krik, Krik, Krik...* he said, still smiling. Was that the bird he was hearing? Or was he playing with the name of his beloved philosopher? I would never want to know the answer to those questions.

MORRISON'S TROUSERS

You know, I pulled on a pair of old Morrison's trousers this morning, having misplaced my own, and that not for the first time either. (I believe I'd lose my own nose if it weren't properly stuck to the front of this face, God help me.) What a perfect fit they were! I'd never have dreamt it, not in a month of Sundays. Such a handsome cut too! And fancy his having the money to splash out on such things, what with that wife of his to keep up, and all those bawling bairns too, one popping out every six months or so. At least, that's how it seemed to me and to Molly, the dearly beloved. Lost track of their names altogether. So did he, I expect. Probably settled for numbers instead.

Oh, he was such a nice man though, so gentle and peace-loving. Never once saw him swat so much as a fly that had settled on his brow. I believe he loved every last thing that lived and moved. Such a saintly man... Such perfect manners – could've been a priest if he'd got the call. I remember the very place we were standing, the very spot in the bar when he told me that. Yes, it was so big-hearted of him, so much like himself, to hand these over, say that I was welcome to them, more than welcome...

That was one thing he never seemed short of, trousers, odd as it may sound. Food, yes. Trousers, no. He had umpteen pairs kept by for best on a Sunday, tweed in the main; pairs for pubbing in; pairs for digging the allotment in, a middling decent corduroy as I recall, not very old ones either, those ones. Pairs for paying his calls in – he just loved to pop round for a natter, any old hour of the day, any excuse for a good old natter. And even a pair or two for doing sweet nothing in, leaning back against Harris' wall, arms folded, watching the larks go by, or squatting down there on his own doorstep beside the road, clutching his stick, that old hazel stick of his...

Molly never took to him all that much, but me and him, we were close as two peas in a pod. She wouldn't have let me have them, oh no, if it had been up to her, but it wasn't... She never knew a thing about it, oh no, not for ages. I stuffed them up the front of this jumper, and walked in the door backwards, waving at nothing at all. Clever, eh?

So here they are then, hugging this waist of mine fast as that bright-eyed young girl up at Killigan's barn dance the other year. I could've seen that one again if I'd troubled, I reckon... Making these old legs of mine look as straight and as handsome and fast off the mark as... what, I wonder? Well, we'll leave that one. Perhaps the truth of it is that there's nothing on earth that's equal to these legs of mine when set off by Dick Morrison's trousers.

It was a grey, blustery old morning, sky full of the glooms, top-coat weather, I remember so well, when she handed them over, thrust them straight at me more like. I'd only come by to pay my respects. Wouldn't have dreamt of it otherwise, not now, with him gone, and even his dog put down for no good reason – excepting her own selfish, brutish nature, I reckon, begrudging its handful of scraps off the table and a spot of its own next to the hearth in the chimney corner, the old place. I swear he'd have turned in his grave if he'd known. He loved it so much, that dog. Stayed up at night when it was having its pups, the man did. There was devotion, unstinting devotion, for you...

As I say, I'd only come by for his sake. And I wasn't in any particular hurry. Thought it best to leave it a day or two, let it blow over. I knew full well I weren't welcome at the wake. Well, I wouldn't be, would I? Still, it doesn't cost a brass farthing to be civil, not in my book. But all she could say for herself, that woman, opening that door of theirs not more than the width of two babies' fingers nails, was:

'Here you go, he left them to you.' Then, as I say, she

thrust them so fast at me that I jumped back, thinking it was maybe her fist coming at me. Wouldn't put it past her, not her. She packed quite a punch, did that woman, according to Morrison. You could fair hear them groan at that chemist, those long suffering weigh scales, when she popped in her penny.

But no, it was his trousers after all coming at me and, of course, being by this time a yard or two back from the door for my own health's sake, playing it cautious, I missed catching them, didn't I, when she went and let go... So, woe is me, there they were, wallowing, the poor things, by the time I reached down – that door was now banged, bolted and barred against me, need I tell you – up to their waist in it and going down further, drowning in that muddy old puddle of water right in front of the door. (No, he'd never got round to that hole, though it's often he'd meant to). Well, I scooped them out best I could, wrung out the worst of it, twisting and twisting – it was a bit of a job, it was, wringing them trousers, so thick was that stuff they were made from, only the best for old Morrison, only the best would do...

No, I never much liked that woman of his, you know. She was always pushing her big nose into this, that and the other, prying out mischief, mischief that wasn't there more likely than not, and if it was... not the sort that would shake a body's hand for pointing it out in the street. Never left a man in peace, that one, neither night nor day. I reckon that's why he was out and about all the time, paying his calls.

So when I was quite done with wringing them out – I had to stop for the sake of my fingers – shooting pains whizzing in all directions – they do say that damp's very bad for the fingers – I smoothed them over the crook of my arm, still dripping a little, and made my way, walking terribly slowly, thinking it over. And it weren't till I got within eyeshot of home that I hit on that difficult, dare-devilish answer: under the jumper and damn the discomfort. And I got them through enemy lines, as you know, without any trouble – thanks to that trick of the waving (old as these hills, that one), and then I went bounding upstairs with them, stuffed them under the sofa...

I guess a whole month must have passed before Molly caught on, but that, no denying, when it happened, was a bit of a... awkward... moment. I come home at tea time – a tea time it certainly was, at the tail end of June, brilliant sun, wisps of cloud in the sky, short-sleeve weather – smacking my lips, thinking of hot buttered toast and of mugs full of sugary tea, two or three, one straight down after another 'cos that's how I like it. My mind was packed full of the stuff, brimming over, with the simple old pleasures of eating and drinking, when I come in that door of mine, smiling and cheerful looking as that clown from old Rogerson's Circus, the one that got nabbed by the coppers for being a bit brazen when he should have known better...

Thirty-six hours he was cooling his heels down there at the station, sobbing in the cold and the chill of his cell, so they said, rattling his bars like a monkey, making an awful old mess of that beautiful make-up... We thought he'd been wronged, every man, Jack and Harry, the whole village, got up a petition, called meetings, quite exciting it was, quite some little kerfuffle... We all chipped in too. Paid the fine. No big problem. Had us some party on what was left over... And I, for one, I still cannot fathom, why, the very day he come out, they pushed him straight over the border. Strange. Ah well...

Yes, I swung through that door of mine, dipping my head so's I wouldn't crack open this tender old pate, no, not so hard-boiled it's not, for all the long years it's been cooking. And it's not that I'm specially long in the leg, but this hovel was built for dwarves, I reckon, dwarves and their smallish babies... And as I come through, I was humming the gayest tune that I knew – Kitty the high-flying curlew, it's called, for your interest, but I was met with, oh God, the stoniest, blackest and scowlingest look I'd been dropped since that time I fell through the front window, still clutching the bottle, and there hangs a sorry old tale that I haven't the time now to touch on, being somewhat alarmed and a little arrested by the sight in the mind of the curl of that lip of hers, and that look in her eye on that – just seconds ago's what it seemed when it happened – blithe and most beautiful day, gone forever...

'Where'd you get these ones?' she said, flapping them out in front of her skirts as if she were taunting some bull in a field, not the sweet-natured lamb she had standing before her, looking so quiet, so innocent-looking, if a little bemused by that question.

'What ones?' I said.

Now, I know to the ear of the average person that question might seem, when weighed in normality's scales, somewhat strange or even a little perplexing. But the point is I needed to say it for the sake of... well... sowing a little confusion. I knew if I managed to sow it, scatter it out before me, even a mite, a small handful or two would suffice, just enough to fill the air that she'd stained with her ranting and raving the angriest tint of blue to be glimpsed in God's spectrum; and then stood back, piously quiet, watching it hang there, calm as a curtain between us, 'cos it's lighter than air is confusion, and handy as mustard gas too, though perfectly harmless. Oh no, I had no wish to harm her.

But it didn't work, not for a tenth of a second or even one hundredth part of that.

'You know full well what I'm speaking of,' she growled, letting her jaw hang slack as a slavering dog's that's run loose from the pound. Then she flapped them out all over again, right in front of my face, stirring the air of that kitchen into a whirlwind's fury, making the dust motes dance in the sunbeams – if there were any sunbeams left to dance at that hour. I fear that she may have dispelled them. All things that were good and beautiful seemed to have bid their adieux – myself exceptin'... 'I'm speakin' of trousers, these trousers, *his* trousers!'

'Whose trousers?' I said it again – only the words were different – but with pitiful little conviction. I knew she'd seen off the confusion. I'd seen it with these eyes, watched how it oozed though the cracks in the floor, walls and ceiling, the split second she'd opened that great gob of hers.

'Morrison's!' she snapped, all fearsome dentures, like some croc rearing its ugly/beautiful head out of a soupy swamp. God help me, I prayed, wishing just then to be nothing more than some tricksy little bird that sits, a puffball of innocence and naivety, on the croc's nose end.

'Lovely cut,' I said, crooking a finger, and conceding defeat in advance of the battle, having had such a vision of blood and carnage when I glimpsed the inside of that mouth of hers, that I dared not pursue it for the sake of the world's health – and my own... 'aren't they, Molly?'

It's a veil of mist that I'll draw over the rest of that evening, but the upshot was that, in spite of all odds, they lingered, malingered, a day or two longer, those trousers, old Morrison's trousers, flung aside though they had been, ingloriously heaped on the floor though they were, directly beneath the mangle, kicked into no shape at all by that black and entirely unfeeling boot of hers, laced, as it always was, way past the ankle. No, nobody touched them or did a single thing about them at all after that, not for ages. They weren't even granted so much as a mention.

Now why was that? I wonder. I think that I know now the answer. She felt sorry, being a niggardly sort, for having despised and condemned a good, hardly worn pair of trousers. I believe that she glanced at them, short, sharp, sidelong glances, over the coming days, and wondered about them. She saw for herself the good, stout, durable cloth they were made from, and took off her hat to the spinners. She observed in her mind's eye those bony, industrious fingers of hers unpicking the seams, making something more beautiful, meaning something more female, of course, from the wreck of those beautiful trousers...

But she didn't. The fact is, whatever the reason, fear, superstition or something, she didn't, and after they'd lain there in state, God knows how long, at the foot of the mangle, God knows how long, from full moon to half moon to crescent, I plucked them up, bold as brass, up from the floor, after dark on a Tuesday evening, and spirited them off to their rightful last home in a topmost tallboy drawer of the marital bedroom. I give them a drawer to themselves all right – in their honour. Way I see it is: what's the fun in being a pair of trousers, classic in cut and cloth, if you can't stretch out your legs and lie a bit comfortable? May as well screw yourself up for a bit of old tat and be buggered. And then again: that drawer was way out of her reach, wasn't it now, Molly being a bit on the dwarfish side, though her build was solid enough...

Did she know where I stowed them? Was she looking? If she did, not a word did she say, not a look did she give me for doing it, and, by and by, maybe a day or two after, – my mind's somewhat hazy – having screwed on my breast plate of valour, I walked out in them, one bright, breezy morning, touch of rain in the air, striding forth boldly, tramping the usual circuit of lanes and more lanes, not once looking over my shoulder. And now I'm standing here in them again, and I don't give a damn for her ravings...

Now I know there are things that are said in these parts about Morrison and the way that he come by his trousers, and it's not just the trousers, I grant you – there's the watches, the number of jewels in his watches, but I never saw nothing of that for myself, not having much time worth the keeping. And it's not just from Molly I've heard them, these tales, oh no, it's from others, but especially the ones that had shunned him, and raised high their glasses, the say, the evening he caught it, full in the neck, that bullet.

And they're calling me fool, in this street, to my face, to my back, friends of mine, former friends, whispering words, telling me: burn them. But for me, I can't do it. They're all that he's left me. It's like burning his memory. And I've also been thinking: how much is there, will you tell me, of God and the Pope and a murderous religion can be wrapped in the cut and the cloth and the hang of a pair of old trousers?

NELLIE'S DEVILS

Nellie kept three enamel buckets – one large and two small – on the upper landing, just beneath the skylight, to catch the drips.

When she lay abed at nights, stiff and straight as a poker, on her left side for luck, listening out for the drips if it was teeming out of doors, the roar of the gas fire that made her toes tingle, rain or shine, or for the devils that, once in a while, ascended and descended the stairs (they stepped up light as a feather, no matter how great a crowd, but still she heard them), it was then she would think of the vicar and boil up again inside herself with anger.

Whenever she looked at this new one, at his crooked teeth, she wished to the bottom of her heart that the old one, her old one, hadn't passed away so early of septicaemia. If he'd asked her – he only had to ask – she would have done for him – instead of that string of brainless, babbling young foreign girls who never kept anything clean and properly laundered, and especially not the hem of his vestments. He kissed her on the hand when the time, always too soon, came to go. He'd been a captain one time in the regular forces.

So when the new vicar came to call, the one with the pointy ears and the squashy blue nose and the cheeks that had been scrubbed red raw, she did her level best to keep him out, but when she looked up, he was always standing there in the corner of the room, smiling down at her, with his thin thumbs circling each other. He must have magicked his way in here, she thought. She even tried to stop herself talking to him, but in no time at all, she heard the words popping out of her mouth of their own accord.

He'd promised to get rid of them – but had he heck! In the old one's day there had been seven only, but now there were seventy-three, and how they all fitted into the one small room, let alone the double bed when it came to sleep, she hadn't a clue. She had pointed them out to him one day, pointed to the seventy-three grinning faces ranged along the pillow there, each one beckoning to her with his own horny finger, and grinning fit to split his brazen face in half. She had even stabbed at them with her stick, but those red faces were as tough as old rubber, she knew from of old. They didn't even flinch – let alone bleed. But what had he said, this new-fangled one with the cheery face? Don't be so silly, Nellie, he'd said, get in and make the seventy-fourth before you catch your death in your night dress. And old Mrs Fletcher downstairs was no better. If you haven't the eyes to see, what in the world's the good of looking?

But for one whole week now they'd stayed away, and Nellie guessed that she knew the reason for it. She had thought to herself: if only I could find out what it is they most dislike, and give it to them or leave it for them or throw it at them. Then, quite by accident, she thought she had. By and by, when the milder weather had come at the end of June, she took the buckets into the bedroom. One went under the bed itself for safe keeping. The second she made into a handy little chair by plonking an old bread board down on top – a perfect circular fit as it turned out. That would do for her nephew to squat on when he came to pay his Thursday call. She didn't much like him sitting on the side of the bed and making it sag with the weight of his great big bottom. No, he could sit on the bucket in the corner and blink up at her from there while she sat pretty in her high bed and shouted at him for wasting his life.

It was what she did with the third bucket that did the trick though. One day in the winter she had dropped and broken her pot in the middle of the night and the bits and pieces got scattered everywhere, not to speak of the pints of her water that she'd mopped up as best she could. Luckily, the next day had been crisp, bright and sunny, so the carpet had dried off in no time. But come the summer she decided, for her old legs' sake, that she'd done with all that trudging up and down stairs, back and forth to the bathroom at dead of night when you never knew who or what you'd meet coming up or down. So the third bucket was the perfect remedy. She'd do it in there – and none would be any the wiser if she kept a little embroidered cloth over it with beads at the edges to keep it taut.

Now she'd always been most particular about her urine in the past. Most particular. If she'd done a little riddle in the night, she'd be carrying it down first thing, having first had a look see that there was nothing abnormal in there. If there's ever anything seriously wrong, that's the first place you'll spot it, her ma's old doctor had told her one time, and she'd told Nellie. It must have been absent-mindedness then that caused her to leave it up there in the bucket for a day or two – or was it three? Nor was her nose quite as sharp as it had been in the old days.

So when Ronald came in that Thursday on the dot of seven, his fingers flew straight up to his nose, clothes-peg-wise, and he near on fell into a dead faint, pulling his face about in the most ridiculous fashion as if he'd been gassed in the trenches like her old father or something. He knew right off what it was because he snatched up the bucket before she'd even had a chance to jump out of her bed and save her own dignity by doing it for him. Still, she couldn't help laughing to herself when he'd gone to see him pull such funny faces. It was a rare enough treat to be made to laugh by Ronald.

That night they all came trooping back, all seventy-three of them. She didn't notice them at first – they were such clever ones with their disguises, standing straight upright, one upon another's shoulders, behind a billowing curtain that never ceased billowing, for example, or lying sidewise in drawers behind the green winter blanket, holding their breath, arms straight down. It wasn't until she slipped into her bed that she found them there already.

At first she pretended not to notice, not to think at all about what was lying there beside her, just imagining to herself that it was maybe a long and stretched-out-thin hot water bottle that was tittering to itself, gurgling in its throat like a drain, and twisting its fingers and toes about like a proper little fidget arse. For a while she made do with the occasional slap – and may even have enjoyed it a little. She was a big one for the party games in her youth, was Nellie. But when the rest of them of a sudden slipped out of the drawers and struck up with the party music on bass drum, triangle and brassy bugles, a sight more rasping than Ronald's had ever been when he was a boy that poked things into people's ears as they were nodding off of an afternoon – just for the fun of it, of course – she set about her business, flailing about with her stick with as much vim and venom as her old bones would muster.

The very last one, a real old stickler for his bed, she pounded and pounded until her sheet was in tatters and the dust from the mattress choking her throat. What an infernal pother! But she got him all right. She chased him round and round the room, out of the door, down the stairs, and right through Mrs Fletcher's part to the front door. And what a good old swipe on the bum she gave him when she caught him wriggling through the letter box! It was well worth the pane of glass or two that came shivering down and woke up old Ma Fletcher, the grumpy old devil. Grumpier than her devils by half, thought Nellie.

She was just settling the sheet around her chin – just like at the barber's, she thought – and getting back her breath from all that running, when the famous thought struck her, the thought about her urine. That while it had been there in the bucket, they'd kept right away, hadn't troubled her once. She laughed to herself to think that an army of devils could be as particular as that Ronald. So she tried it again – no harm, was there, it being a Friday, and Ronald six whole days away? She'd have no trouble keeping old Ma Fletcher out, and if she didn't stop her poking her nose into other folks' affairs by any chance, she'd just throw a little fit in front of her very eyes, and that would set her running off back where she came from.

So up jumps Nellie, carefully rolls back the linen cover, counting the beads, every last one, to make sure none had gone missing (for hadn't an old preacher once told her mother that beads on dresses and hat brims and such like were the devil's sweeties?), and does her a good, long, splashy riddle, quite enjoying the drifting aroma, it being her own. She swirls it about a bit to guess how much, and thinks to herself that she'd better add another dollop in the morning for good measure.

Then off she pops into a most contented sleep.

The very moment she wakes, and without even opening her eyes, she listens out for them – a tiny, tell-tale rustling, for example, or the smallest and driest and briefest of barks – like a dog that's got a chicken bone stuck in its throat two or three streets away. No, nothing at all to disturb her but the thinnest pencil of sunlight, chock full of dust, falling and swirling across her pillow. Their doing as well, she thinks, for had those creatures not disturbed the curtains when they'd jumped down from each other's shoulders and given her a cheeky bow – just like those acrobats she saw in that circus one time?

Then, all of a sudden, she hears the bell tolling, rattling her head, and, by golly, she thinks, it's a Sunday already! And what ever happened to that Saturday I was expecting? Did those devils make off with that one as well? Not that she really minds very much, for now comes the happiest moment of all: choosing the hat. For the cupboards are chock full of them, and many not even released from the box they were bought in – like beautiful birds forever imprisoned in their cages. Some bottle-green, in the shape of a pork pie, she examines, and others the colour and the crispness of meringues that are done to a tee in the oven. Sweet-looking enough to be eaten whole, she thinks, smacking her lips.

Not wishing to shock old Ma Fletcher and others, she plucks out the white straw one with the brim that half covers her face. Now she can see and not be seen — by troublesome humans or devils, she thinks. And then again her face in the mirror reminds her so much of that picture of Saturn with its rings on the old tea cards, the most beautiful of planets. Last but not least is the Prayer Book to keep her from harm, and that she keeps in the drawer, upper left, of the desk that her father bequeathed her, alongside his teeth.

At last I am ready! she thinks, as she tweaks at the brim of the hat, and clutches the book to her bosom — then, looking down, she laughs fit to fall flat on her face to see herself still in her nightie...

In she comes last, shunning the Prayer Book that's offered, shaking her own in the face of that foolish Mavis, ever forgetful. Old Ma Fletcher had kept her place, and for that she is grateful. One time she went in, and seeing a stranger where she should have been, ran right out again, shaking with anger and grief. The thing was the stranger had looked the very spit of her.

Such a hush is there in God's house that the only sound is of Nellie's creaking shoes making their way to the place that is hers near the altar. Why, there are hundreds here today, she thinks, surprised, to herself, having banked on the usual twenty. Down she goes on her knees and presses her thumbs to her eyeballs, making the lightning fork in the darkness in front of her eyes. Avenge me, almighty, she whispers, please murder the lot of them. Then she sees in her mind's eye a thousand black crosses raised up, and a thousand red devils hung from them, weeping and wailing and grinding their toothless gums. But it is not just the hands and the feet that they're nailed by – there's a good, hefty bolt through each neck for good measure. And Nellie herself is standing there, staunch in her wellies, for a mighty river of blood is flowing past her. And Christ Jesus, also dry-footed, is standing beside her and asking: is it well done, Sister Nellie?

At that she smiles and she nods, rapping her head on the pew in front like some stranger knocking. Then it is that Ma Fletcher fetches her a good old stab in the ribs, and Nellie swings round to face her, eyes glaring, lips quivering. She sees only a forest of legs, for they're all on their feet now and singing, heartily singing. Then she cries out, fist jamming her mouth, at...not the legs themselves, but their colour, and the fact that they have no shoes or nothing...

Quickly she scrambles between them, pushing and beating her way to the aisle, flailing about with her Prayer Book. She runs to the door, with others pursuing. Some snatch at her hat – and now they have it! Let them keep it, she thinks, spitting over her shoulder. Rather a hat than a soul, for all its beauty. Out she goes, running hell for leather through the church yard, hearing the pack of them baying at her back.

At last – long last! – she is safe in her room again, where she slumps to the floor, exhausted. Now she stares full in the face of the truth that none can deny: that nowhere, but nowhere, is safe out of doors if God does not reign in his house any longer. Not the street, she thinks. Not a neighbour's house, she thinks. Not even the staircase that winds down to Ma Fletcher's, for there is no denying the goings on up and down these stairs at the minute, she thinks, listening...

She throws herself at the door, turns the key in its lock, and breathes freer. She dandles it in her fingers, then drops it into the bucket, watching its wavy yellow reflection. And, knowing full well what's best to do next, she drags out the bucket from under the bed and drives out a stream to the very last drip. Then she places it under the window, and ties two knots in her curtains. Next she pulls out the drawers and flings out the blankets. Where else might they hide? she thinks, scouring walls, floor and ceiling with her eyes...

Under the bed! Her heart misses a beat at the thought they are there already, a string of them sitting cross-legged, hunch-shouldered, and holding their noses. But no, not a hint or a whisper, for she crawls right under, from side to side, eyes skinned for the least sign of movement in the misty, dusty murk of that underbed world...

Out again, she lies flat on her bed, opening the Prayer Book across her chest like a breastplate. How long exactly she lies there, staring about her, fitfully dozing, starting awake, she does not know. Even the clock has stopped. But what is a clock to me? she thinks, stretching over to turn it down flat on its face. One time she hears knocks on the door, soft, and then louder, and a voice, two voices, calling – one high and one low. She smiles to herself, tight-lipped, thinking: what have they to teach me of wolves in sheep's clothing?

Late on it is – for the light is now falling – that she opens a tin of rice pudding – one of the twenty or so she keeps in a cupboard – and spoons it in, greedy, having quite forgotten her hunger in all that unworldly excitement. She stretches, yawning, feeling most delicious amidst the peace of her seclusion – and fights her way into her nightie. Straight off she goes with a smile on her lips, thanking her lord for the natural cause of her deliverance.

She awakes, in the dark, to the certain sound of water splashing and turning – and the tiniest tinkle of laughter. Surely it cannot be, she thinks, shifting her legs to the ground, and easing herself off the bed as quietly as she can manage in her stiffness. She tiptoes across to the window, and there, by the moonlight, she sees it, a baby one, swimming and plunging and tumbling in the inches of her water. And her heart goes out to it. She plunges her hand in and combs the water for it, all the while gurgling and cooing. And it lets itself lie in her hand, and even smiles up at her, pushing its tail through her fingers. She raises it, kisses its brow, showers it under the tap, and then dries it on her nightie. And even as she watches, it grows and grows until she has not the strength to hold it. So she sets it down on its sturdy young legs, and admires it for a handsome boy, if a little surly, but still growing...

And, arm in arm, they skip back to her bed.

THE RABBIT AND THE HARE: A CRISIS OF IDENTITY

The rabbit was running here, there, everywhere, left, right, left, spurting, dodging, weaving. In blind fear it ran, behind the clattery dustbin, beside the arrow-straight canal, out again into the open breathingness of the field. It was running in fear of itself, in fear of what it had become. It had caught a glimpse of itself in a window as it ran – had it ever before run through an open street, with all those terrible, pestering, blundering feet!

How had it happened? How had it grown such ears? It was running away from its ears, from the fear of its ears, which had grown far, far too long. These are not rabbit's ears! it was telling itself as it ran and it ran, through city and countryside, on soft ground or hard, through lush forests of long-combed grass or cold, pinching alleyways, into the teeth of driving rain, or beaten down on, without a scrap of mercy, by the blazing sun. These are not my ears! These are far too long to be rabbit's ears...

The hare was standing poised and tall and quivery-ready at the top of the hill, letting the wind blow its boundless energies through long legs and tight haunches, which shuddered in excitement. It was ready. It had never been so ready. It took one leap and then again, a mighty, soaring arc in the air, bouncing, bounding, soaring. Long and long were its hare-strides, perfectly sculptural in their curvature.

And then something happened. The leaps begin to grow shorter, the legs weaker and not quite so high-bounding. The abundant energies seemed to be seeping away. The hare's head felt cold and small and exposed. He came to a small puddle of water, and into it he stared, in horror he stared, at his greatly diminished and ever diminishing ears. What had happened to his glorious ears? Who had stolen the majesty of his ears?

What has happened to my wondrous ears? wailed rabbit and hare in unison, a thousand miles apart, though so close-knitted in their sorrow.

HAND IN HAND

Were we not hand in hand again? Is that not how I always think of it – when I think of it at all? Let us be truthful. I think of it often. I am never not thinking about it.

I took him back there, and I showed him the room. There was no room. There was merely empty air. No stairs to be climbed. No doors to be opened. No bed to be slept in. No human fug. No uproarious untidiness. No thrillingly quiet aftermaths to be contemplated.

Is this where Gérard lived? you asked me, spitefully. Gérard had barely figured at all – until he entirely engulfed us. It was where we *all* lived, I replied. Then you left me. You blinked and you left me, and I was sitting, once again, in this small London garden of ours, worrying about tomato blight, and the triffid-like creep of the courgette plants. Evening was coming on. It was November again. How many more Novembers, that most hateful of months? Each November, I shrivel a little more. Soon I will be nothing at all.

Your story is not my story, not quite. My story is not yours, not quite. I am a pillar of salt. You are a squat jar of Dijon mustard. When we sit beside that canal in Venice – Fondamenta Ormesini – and stare down into the dark, slow-shifting, polluted waters, your shadow jinks a little, merges into mine, separates. I like it like that, two becoming one, one becoming two again. I would freeze-frame it like that for the future's sake. Venice is what it always must be to us, and as it never will be again.

That worst of our mornings (am I not exaggerating? Were there not far too many for this one to be singled out for special attention? No matter), you had turned on me like a half-starved dog. *You are not famous. You are merely very well known. There is that fine distinction.* Those were your words. I laid down my bow on its taffeta cushion, and stared at you over the music stand. I said nothing. I let my eyes do all the saying. You always hated that, my saying nothing. You hated my silence. You always wanted the world to be filled with words, amusing words, and I would listen, suitably amused, or turn away and think of something – or someone – else. Do I not have the right to think of someone else? Are my thoughts not as free as the wind? You hated me when I said that. Then I did say something. *And what have you ever done?* I asked him, and he visibly shrank in front of me like a child's balloon freshly pin-pricked. I knew so well how to needle him. Long years of practised retaliation.

We made the room together, bit by bit, as we had always done, in this city or that. Venice. Paris. London. You were more handy than me. You could see ahead. You could imagine an outcome. I, by comparison, crept along. I am good for the present moment, its freshness, its sweetie-suckableness, its freedom, its – well – overwhelming immediacy. How one lapses so readily into the platitudinous! I would slip into the kitchen for a coffee and the surface-sugary delights of a *langue de chat*. I would sit there, watching the leaf of the calendar gently a-flutter against the wall. Each leaf would offer up a different scene – all very traditional, of course. The Moulin-Rouge in its heyday. The Tour Eiffel under construction. The neo-classical pomp of the facade of the Madeleine. Yes, we always kept the kitchen window open, even by as little as a slivver, in that one-room apartment of ours just off the Rue Lepic. There is no life without air. There is no life without those rising noises from the courtyard, the rumbling of the *poubelles* – in and out, out and in – the gentle up-driftings of acrid cigarette smoke, all those furtive human murmurations whose veiled meanings I would strive to draw in, always failing, of course.

You would catch me standing beside the window,

staring across at Gérard, who would be posed there in profile, so sleek, so vital, so youthful, in his yellow cashmere sweater. Was he fiddling with the *cafetière* again? Is that what his slender fingers were working at, at waist height needless to say? I smiled to myself. I am such a sucker for my own jokes. One can only imagine.

I am working, and *you are idling and leering*, you would say as you entered, blunderingly (as was your wont), *you lazy little toss-pot you*. Why did you always insist on speaking so noisily, and especially in the smallest of spaces? Even when I buried you, you shouted words of exasperation from the coffin – heard only by myself, needless to say. I put my finger to my lips. And then I transferred it to yours. Pulpy. Pink. Quivery. You reddened in exasperation. You turned on your heel, still clutching a screwdriver. How your knuckles were shining!

I had always wanted to own a Courbet. It had never happened. Had one been bequeathed to me? I watched myself opening the box which contained it. A mahogany box, exquisitely lined with royal-blue velvet. Why a box though? Why should a small painting by Courbet be stifled inside a mahogany box? The better – the more sensible – question might be: why is the small detailing of dreams always so improbable? Does the creator of dreams not care enough? Anyway, that was my favourite dream, to receive that magical gift of an exquisite Courbet...

I was thinking of that dream as we tried to find a place best suited to our expensive reproduction of *L'Origine du Monde*. Over the *cheminée*, of course, where the mirror would once have hung, that cherished spot where self-regard is naturally inclined to come to rest and then to marvel, lingeringly. Female pudenda defined Paris for us – due to the additional fact, of course, that we lived on the corner of the Boulevard Rochechouart, in the very heart of Pigalle.

What exactly do you do all day? Accusation. Counter-accusation. Who is asking whom? We are standing face to face. Your breath smells of mint. I smirk. My face is tilted up towards yours. You harumph and turn on your heel. Seconds later, the outer door is slammed, and I am raising my bow again. I hear the clatter of your heels across the cobbles down below. Curious, ever curious, I lean from the balcony and watch you go, that quick turn left down towards the boulevard. Rue Lepic. How it touches me to remember that name! You do not look back. You have never looked back. Your collar is turned up. You look like a man with a mission to be someone, to go somewhere. Where though? And with whom if not with me?

I sigh. You are fading again. You arrive with such an intensity of feeling, and then you fade as if you have given up on me. The sun has dipped behind the garden wall. A chill is coming on. Oh, these long Sunday afternoons, quite pleasingly alone in a London garden! I jest. I amuse myself.

The day of your burial. It was so long and so cold. It began so early. I stared for hours at the wall. I watched it lighten, emerge from out of the dark, so painfully slowly, as the sun rose. I both thought of you and did not think of you. I had wanted you to leave so often. And now you had left, once and for all. A single telephone call had given me all the bald facts. A careless stepping out into the road – you never knew whether to look to the left or the right when in London, you were never at home here. Were you ever at home anywhere? When we first met, you had looked like a young man adrift on the waters, chancing his life, quick, furtive. When you drank, you always raised your glass so quickly, as if the gesture had to be over and done in order to clear a little space for the next one. What was that to be? You never seemed to know. I had to plan your life for you, sit you down.

Now you were not so much sitting as lying, peacefully lying. Were you at peace though? Were you not a-jitter in there, in that box, beating with your fists on the lid for an explanation? It felt like that to me. Outwardly though, there was silence. You were not, for once, a public embarrassment.

The three of us are sitting around the table. The feast is over. A few stray chicken bones have escaped from the plate. You lift the wishbone with your little finger and, raising it, offer it to both of us, swinging it slowly from side to side between the two of us, another of your pretty little taunts. Gérard smiles and waves it away. He wants to have nothing to do with it. He knows what you are up to, what you have always been up to. You jab it in his direction – you hate being ignored. You hate it when your little games are spurned or swept aside as so much foolishness.

Meanwhile, I have risen up onto my feet, gently lifted the salad bowl from the table, and begun to turn towards our most tiny of Parisian kitchens, where all is always to be done. The old copper pans are stacked in wild ziggurats of upheapings. There is still a smell of candle smoke trapped in there. Out in the courtyard I hear them again, the boys down below. They are kicking a can about. A great cry goes up at my back. I turn. Gérard has hold of the larger segment of the wish bone. And now you are falling forwards onto his neck, planting a great kiss there. I watch your movement towards him, the graceful arc that you made. You could have made so much of your life. I can only smirk. I can only join in the fun.

It is never too late to refresh my imaginings.

LOVE. LOVE. LOVE.

For a little while it lasts, and then it goes away. Everything is always the same. Nothing remains. Nothing stays here long enough for me to love it. Even as I approach, it disappears.

She lifts up the saucer, and smells the fish. Disgusting. She looks for the matches above the cooker. All gone. She stares at the photograph of the two of them together, he, standing, in his uniform, she, seated, in her best finery, hat such an almighty flourish of ribbons and bibbons and roses, practically drowning in it. All gone too.

Except she, she thinks, *this* one. She prods at her chest. How ribby she feels. Like a xylophone. *She* malingers still. She sighs just to think of it, and then pushes her arms into her coat, catching her thumb in the tear, making it a little bigger.

Cold, wheedling wind, harrying, at her back, as she makes her way. Always so little to be done, and so much time in which to do it, the slow walk downhill, and then the even slower walk back uphill, pulling her trolley behind her, empty now, hardly much fuller by and by. The pleasure of the small ads are what she is after, in the window of the newsagent's. A lawnmower, needing some attention, £5 or best offer considered. Respectable cleaning lady wanted, bring own cloths, three hours a week. Ford Cortina. One careful owner. See it to believe it.

She stares at herself in the window. See it to believe it, she is thinking to herself, the comedy of her own self looking at what remains of her now. Her hair, flat to her head, has not been permed in months. Who would care to look at her anyway? What would be the point when she does not go anywhere to be seen, and when no one visits, not any more? At least her dentures are in. She makes the rounds of them with her dry tongue. Yes, firmly in.

She watches the notes and the coins being counted out at the post office, the speed with which it is done. She can barely keep up; the mental arithmetic is not what it was. Blondie slides it across, the kindly postmistress in her bits of scarves, through the little gap at the bottom of the window, the cellophane bag, heavy with her pension, weekly. More than enough. What is there to spend it on?

Once back, she carefully closes the kitchen curtains against prying eyes. Now begins the task. She takes out the little cellophane bags, all of them, and lines them up in a row across the table. Electricity. Gas. Children. Holidays. Extras. She pops a coin or two in here and a note in there, and then she makes the calculations on paper, adding it all up, bringing herself up to date, licking her lips as she leans over to give it her full attention. The children are too old now, but she gives them their portion all the same. There's no one who doesn't need money. She doesn't take the holidays – who would she holiday with? How did she ever walk on sand? – but it is easier to continue with the old routines than to stop. There is something reassuring about it all. Setting the world to rights.

Love. Love. Love. On the radio.

THE PUZZLE

I am very particular about the little things. Pins. Paper clips. Even small balls of dust. I like to tidy them away, in heaps. I do like routines, you see. What would a day be without its routines?

There's always so much to be done, so much crowding in on you. A day is barely enough to contain it all. Summer is best – when the days are long. Funny how you feel inclined to close your eyes when darkness descends. The answer is to keep on top of it, and then it won't overwhelm you. I wake at five, bright as a new pin, and I look about, in the half-light – the bedroom curtains are thin enough to admit a little light, which pleases me – in order to reassure myself that nothing has gone astray.

Nothing ever has gone astray. I always see to that before I put out the light, straightening the ornaments on the shelf, polishing my darling little ballerina until I can practically see my face in her, so slender, so beautiful, so fragile – I dread the thought of breaking the dear – making sure that all the drawers are closed. I do so hate a half-open drawer, and all that it tells you about the messiness of other people's lives. Dirt and messiness – they are life's biggest scourges.

Mavis arrives at ten on a Thursday morning, and I make her a cup of Nescafé, not too hot though. She so easily burns her lips. She sucks at it to test just how hot it is, the most dreadful slurping noise, that I pretend to ignore. I can hear her approaching because she shuffles her feet, and then she clears her throat once or twice before knocking – always so gently – on the door. She is such a timid soul, and even more so now that she is on her own. She does not cope very well. She cries without warning. I keep a new box of Kleenex out on the kitchen table so that I am well prepared. She knows she can reach out for it. She doesn't have to be asked.

I bring it out on a tray – I don't touch it between visits – and set it down between us. She brightens when she sees it. She sniffs, and tosses her head, as if to clear it of all that misery. And then she stares down – hard – at the jigsaw puzzle, that part-made picture, surrounded by an untidy strew of heaped pieces. She looks from pieces to picture, picture to pieces. I watch her, fondly. She's like a twitchy little bird. I buy them from the charity shop because we run through so many. Mavis is much quicker than you would think at spotting what goes where. I do it to please her, to distract her from herself. I wouldn't exactly say that my mind is on it. She loves the challenge of a big church especially, a church with a great spire, set in a landscape – Salisbury Cathedral, for example, which turned up in August, in a great big brute of a cardboard box. Five hundred pieces, I recall. She roared through it. I couldn't get over her pleasure. I felt I had done something for her. I had to re-fill the plate of biscuits, more than once. She just didn't seem to notice that she was eating them. It's a good job I have a bit of an occupational pension.

Goodbye, Mavis, see you next Thursday as usual, I said to her on the doorstep. She usually scuttles off when she hears me say those words, but that week she lingered there. Her eyes were brimming with tears of pleasure.

It has been such a happy morning, she said. I feel replete with good memories of happy days, she said. Good, I replied, good. I touched her gently on her bony shoulder. And still she stood there, smiling up at me, head, slightly trembling, tilted to one side, as if she was staring at a dream of me. She's such a little runt of a creature. Never washes her hair. A slightly rancid smell about her.

It is so good to be of some use.

ANNA'S PURSE

Yes, John made the shelves in there – from odds and ends. He was such a practical man, so very good with his hands...He loved that Boy's Brigade, lived for it. I think he would have done anything for them – within reason. I once teased him by saying that he'd spent more time teaching little boys to tie knots and light fires than he ever had with me. Well, he must have done, mustn't he? I wasn't lying. Difficult to change the habits of a lifetime, I suppose.

Don't get me wrong though. They loved him as well, make no mistake. I think that cup meant more to him than almost any other gift. He didn't even open half of the wedding presents, naughty man. Just left it to me – all the thank you letters too. I suppose that sort of thing means less when you're older. Not as though we were teenagers...It was the first thing to go up on the mantelpiece after we moved here. There we were, surrounded by boxes and boxes, wondering what ever to do next. Suddenly, he reached down, plucked it out – he remembered exactly where he'd packed it! – and up it went. How ever did you know? I said, marvelling. Then he pointed to the blue cross. He'd chalked a cross on the side of the box. How ingenious! I thought. By this time, he'd picked it up again and was rubbing it on his sleeve, shining it up for all it as worth. That cup was like a baby to him.

I think that's the only thing he regretted about moving here – severing the links with his old troop. Not that he'd been an active member for many years. He so loved doing those inspections though and handing out the certificates and badges and things. He was like a child when he received a letter from them in the post. He'd get all dressed up days before and just stand there in front of the mirror, adjusting his cap and whistling the old marching tunes under his breath. Funny. Hmm. Sweet.

Did I tell you we once thought of living in the annex? Don't you think the fire places are absolutely charming? So charming. And I do so love those old sinks. They're so strong and so big. Take any number of double sheets. I hate the stainless steel ones. Poor, flimsy things. My nephew David sleeps there when he comes – about once a month.

Yes, John just came out with it one day. He'd just put the staircase in. He was a marvel with his hands... He turned to me – he was just standing there, holding his cup of tea – piping hot as usual – and he said: Anna, why don't we go on holiday to the annex? We laughed and laughed, looking up the stairs. We could have done too. That's what really tickled me. He was such a funny man. Not to everyone though. Oh no. He took that Boy's Brigade ever so seriously. He'd really earned that cup. He did look so comical in those khaki shorts though – I never told him so to his face. He would have been terribly hurt, the poor dear.

I'm almost certain that's where it is. You see, it's the very last place I remember having it. I'd just come in – I remember it so well – clutching the shopping bag in one hand and the purse in the other. I always used to be very particular about that purse. Always carried it about in my hand. I was so terrified of losing it. It wasn't the money I cared about. What's money? It comes and goes. No, it was the purse itself. Nor was it the only thing he'd ever given me. He used to shower presents on me – at first. So gallant. Very proper though. He never overstepped the mark. He didn't even kiss my cheek until the evening of the day he proposed to me. A Sunday. Showery. It was heavenly when it came though. So gentle. So tender. Then he gave me the purse, all wrapped up in a piece of rather crumpled tissue paper. Men. There was no ceremony. He was very embarrassed about it if anything. He just said – I'll remember his words to my dying day – you may be needing one of these, Anna. Then he sort of pushed it at me – not roughly, mind you. As if he wanted to get it over and done with as quickly as possible so that he could move on to other matters. He turned away and started examining the carpet, disturbing the pile with his foot. His face was red as a beetroot. I could have warmed my hands at it. I didn't say anything though – except, 'thank you, John,' of course. He didn't even look at me after it was unwrapped, not for ages.

It was a marvellous thing though, unlike any other purse I'd ever seen in my life. Brown and mottled – like the skin of some rare snake. I couldn't stop running my finger over it, wondering. Turning it about in my hand. At last I opened it and there, tucked inside, was a crisp ten-shilling note. My mouth fell open. So much money! Just then he looked up and spoke. I thought you might want to buy yourself a hat for the wedding, he said quietly. He was smiling at me now, so I didn't feel so awkward leaning across and kissing him.

How I treasured that purse, his very first gift! He bought me so many different things after that, many of them bigger and more expensive looking than the purse, but it was always the purse that I treasured most. It went everywhere that we went. It was my constant companion. I never asked him where he bought it from. I can't imagine that it was English though. There was a little square of leather sewn inside on which the name of the maker was printed – in gold. LUGONI, it read. Just that. Italy? I wondered.

I remember I had it with me, I was clutching it, the day I came in with the shopping in the other hand and heard him calling down from the annex. Not my name – just crying out as if he was in trouble. I dropped the shopping bag on the floor by the door, ran upstairs as fast as my legs would carry me – how my heart was beating! – turned into our bedroom, and yanked open the door to the annex. I knew that's where he'd been calling from. He was decorating it, preparing it for our holiday – or the guests. When I reached the top of the staircase – his staircase – I could see him stretched out on the floor. He was still holding the paint brush in his hand. I remember feeling annoyed to see the white streaks of paint on the floor boards. How stupid of me! How unkind! How selfish!

I must have put it down somewhere. I don't think the ambulance men would have taken it. They were so kind to both of us. One of them held my hand in the back of the ambulance all the way to the hospital. A very big man, much bigger than John, with a beaming, ruddy face. He was such a comfort. He even found me a chair in the casualty department and squeezed my hand when he said goodbye. Definitely not the sort to steal an old lady's purse. They took John away from me as soon as we arrived. They dumped him on a trolley like a sack of potatoes and drew screens round him. It was ever so hot in that place, so hot that I must have nodded off because the next thing I remember was Margaret peering down at me, her face very close to mine. She made me jump. Fancy coming that close! What ever's the matter? I said when I opened my eyes. I didn't mean to sound cross with her – but I must have done, I suppose. Harold is waiting outside in the car, she said, slipping her arm through mine. I didn't budge. I told her I wasn't leaving without John. She sighed and said it wouldn't do any good to wait because they were keeping him in a special ward overnight that wouldn't admit visitors. Don't they know I'm his wife? I said. He just needs to be quiet, she said. He needs to be on his own for a little while so that they can examine him and get to the bottom of it. I hummed and haahed a bit, but I went with her eventually. The doctors must know what's best for him, I thought. They're the specialists.

I didn't sleep a wink that night, not a wink. I've never slept well at Margaret's. Something to do with Harold, I think. We've never got on. He always looks so gloomy and depressed all the time. Never a word for the cat. Margaret couldn't be more different. How ever did she come to marry him? It was Margaret who suggested that we move from Weston-Super-Mare to the south coast. Just in case anything happened to any of us, she said. John thought that was a good idea. Did he have a premonition that he would die first? Who knows... Perhaps Harold resented our living there. Perhaps he thought that we complained about him behind his back, told tales. I wouldn't dream of doing such a thing. Margaret thought the world of him. John and I thought the world of Margaret. We didn't want to spoil anyone's happiness. He never seemed pleased to see us though, so we spent as little time as possible with them. Margaret and I kept in touch by telephone instead. We might as well have still been living in Weston-Super-Mare.

He didn't say anything about John's accident. I kept glancing up at his face in the rear-view mirror, expecting him to smile at least, to say some comforting word or something. No, his face was stony, expressionless. When he looked at me, he seemed to stare right through me as if I was a ghost. Margaret was a dear, of course. She brought me a cup of Horlicks in bed and told me not to worry. She said everything would turn out for the best. And still I didn't sleep. But it wasn't poor John I was thinking about all that night. It wasn't even morose Harold – though I could hear his rumbling snores through the wall. It was the purse. I was fretting about that purse.

It wasn't until I'd got back to Margaret's that I'd noticed it was missing. And when I realised, I burst into tears – just like that. Margaret had to go back to the house to fetch my night clothes. I insisted, I absolutely insisted, on going with her. She said I must rest, but I told her that I wouldn't rest until until I had it in my hand again. She drove this time. Harold didn't even offer.

I was trembling when I got into the car, shaking like a leaf. She told me not to be so silly, and that calmed me down a bit. I closed my eyes and listened to the swish of the windscreen wipers. She asked me for the front door key before I got out, and I handed it over without a murmur. Like a child. I hadn't the strength to do anything. I could easily have cried again – but I knew I mustn't for Margaret's sake. I turned to look at the cottage again. The windows looked so blank and dark – as if no one had ever lived there. I couldn't even see the geranium in the window. It didn't seem to be our cottage any more.

I followed her up the path, hanging back, nervous to go in again. Fearful of what I'd find there – or wouldn't find. Where shall we start then? she said briskly, turning to face me in the hall. She was doing her best to cheer me up, the dear thing. She even switched on the light. I didn't answer. I just began to walk up the stairs. Margaret came on behind, with a steadying hand on my shoulder. Perhaps she thought I'd faint and fall back down or something. I couldn't hurry for the life of me – not even for the purse. I'm a very good walker normally – always have been. John and I used to walk miles along the Promenade, back and forth, arm in arm, just watching the sea. It never looked the same two days – two minutes! – together. He was a powerful swimmer too. You had to be in the Boys' Brigade. Not that we swam much at our age. The stories he told me though...

Even walking seemed beyond me that night. I could hardly manage my own stairs. I had to let my left foot draw level with my right before I could take another step up. I was really feeling my age. I've never felt that old since... The paint brush was still on the floor, of course, in its pool of clotted paint. I didn't feel cross about that any more, thank goodness. Just blank. It was almost as if someone had given me a drug to numb my feelings. Margaret picked it up and put it on the step ladder, the ladder he must have fallen from...

We searched high and low. We scoured every inch of that floor. Then we went back downstairs, and Margaret emptied out the contents of my shopping basket onto the dining room table. Half a pound of margarine. Fish fingers. A packet of John's favourite biscuits. But no purse. Not a sign of it. It had just vanished.

Margaret made us a cup of tea. She wouldn't let me lift a finger to help. Go and sit down, Anna, she said. Please try and relax. We don't want two invalids in the family now, do we? One's more than enough to be going on with. I nodded and went into the sitting room.

As soon as I sat down, I noticed his reading glasses on the chair opposite, his chair. They were open. He was so careless with spectacles, always sitting on them and having to buy new ones. The times I must have warned him to put them back in the case. The times I've stood in that doorway and waved it at him. The case always survived. Cheap things, things you don't care much about, always do. I picked them up and plonked them down on the mantelpiece – out of harm's way. Funnily enough, I hadn't folded them up and put them away either. I left them just as he'd left them – open.

Margaret came bustling in with the tray. She'd made the tea in the best china cups. Why? I said, feeling a bit hurt. Why not? she replied. I don't remember a single thing about the journey back to hers. Perhaps I fell asleep in the car. I think it had stopped raining by then. But what a night it was, such a restless, sleepless night. And that was the first of many. Even sleeping tablets didn't help. They just made me feel very drowsy during the day, too drowsy to do anything but sit in a chair with my eyes closed. I even let Margaret hoover around my feet. I felt like a vegetable. And still Harold didn't say a word to me. Whenever I opened my eyes, he seemed to be hidden behind his newspaper. It was as though he didn't want to talk to me. What could I have done wrong?

Late in the afternoon of that first day, Margaret came in to say that we could visit him that evening. They'd finished operating on him, and now he'd been moved to another ward. He was out of danger, she said. Visiting hours were between six-thirty and eight. I asked her if they'd told her what had been the matter, and she said they hadn't, but I wasn't sure she was telling me the truth. Margaret's never been a very good liar. She tends to look shifty and embarrassed. Sometimes her voice even goes croaky. She won't look you in the eye. I didn't press her though. I'd see for myself soon enough, I thought.

Harold came too. I think Margaret must have told him to. They didn't say a single word to each other on the journey. That made me feel very guilty. I made a resolution there and then to tell her that I would be leaving the following morning no matter how I found him. After all, I'd lived on my own for most of my life – before John and I met. It wasn't something new. I was perfectly able to do for myself. I didn't want to come between them. Anyway, she was only a telephone call away if I really needed her.

As I had expected, Harold stayed in the car with his newspaper. We had to wait around in the corridor outside the ward for about twenty minutes, we and two other people, two old men. They weren't together, I don't think. They never spoke. One of them munched sandwiches. Someone pushed past us with an oxygen cylinder, someone in a brown coat. He was in such a hurry that he almost ran over Margaret's foot. He was whistling a tune that I half recognised. I hoped the cylinder wasn't for John.

He was lying on his side with his eyes closed. His head had been shaved. It took all my self-control not to burst into tears and walk out when I saw that he'd lost his beautiful head of wavy grey hair.

I loved it so much. Margaret took my hand in hers. She must have known what I was thinking because she said: It'll grow again, dear, in no time at all. You'll see...

He was wearing a sort of funny muslin cap on his head, rolled up at the edges. And then there were the two tubes...

When I saw them, I looked away, then down at the little bunch of flowers I was holding in my hands, his favourites. I should have asked for a vase or an old cup without a handle or something else to put them in. I think I may even have left with them.

I looked at him just once more – as we were getting up to leave. A nurse was standing behind us, talking in a loud and cheerful voice. We were the last. He was still breathing evenly through his mouth, blowing out his lips occasionally. He couldn't possibly have breathed down his nose because there were tubes up there as well. The saddest thing was that his breathing sounded exactly as it did when he was lying beside me in bed asleep. I could have closed my eyes and imagined it, but I resisted. I think that was the sensible thing to do.

To my surprise, Harold wasn't sitting at the wheel like a sentinel when we came out. He was standing at the roadside with his hands in his pockets, watching the cars go by. As soon as he saw us approaching, he got in again though. I told Margaret later that evening that I was going back home in the morning. At first she seemed very upset, but when she saw the determination in my eyes, she said I should go back if that's what I really wanted. I said I was sure it was – and squeezed her hand.

In fact, there were two sets of daily visiting hours – between one and three in the afternoon, and the period in the evening. I had to catch two buses to get to the hospital, but I was determined not to accept their offers of help. It wasn't fair on them – and so expensive. Margaret usually visited on a Friday, Friday evening, and then she came back for a cup of tea and a piece of Madeira cake. He was like that for ten years, breathing quietly on his side, the left side or the right, depending upon how the nurses had decided to arrange him after they'd examined his bed sores. He never once opened his eyes or said anything when I was there. If he did when I was absent, no one ever told me. I'm sure they would have. The worst thing was his hair, his beautiful hair, never grew back. Luckily, I had a lock of it in a tin. Ten years and two months to the day – it was a tumour, by the way – he died peacefully during the night. I got the shock of my life when Harold smiled at me at the crematorium.

When I got back home on that first day without him, there was only one thing on my mind: the purse, to find the purse. I started in the annex, of course. I moved everything out, shifting all that furniture from room to room. When the first room, the one in which he'd fallen, was entirely empty, I decided to try underneath the floor boards. For some reason I imagined that it might be under there. I knew that his tools were in the scullery and that the bag was very heavy. I managed to drag it to the bottom of the stairs, and from there I carried them up, one by one, in my arms: the hammers, the two saws, screwdrivers, hand drill, even the wood files. I'd seen him use all these things from time to time. I was sure it wasn't beyond me to use them as well. He would teach me, his spirit would teach me. I knew he wanted me to find the purse just as much as he did.

It was striking three by the church clock when I gashed my finger on the edge of the saw. The sight of all that blood frightened me. It also brought me to my senses. It reminded me just how utterly exhausted I was – and how dirty. I clumsily bandaged my finger, ran a bath – a cold bath because I had quite forgotten to switch on the immersion heater – and crawled into bed, shivering, just as the dawn chorus was starting. How I hated those birds that night! They seemed to be taunting me for losing the purse, the most treasured gift he had ever given me. It was so unlike me to hate them. I love all animals and birds usually – except seagulls. I make an exception for seagulls. Seagulls are such greedy bullies. One morning John put out bread crumbs for the wrens on an old cracked saucer that we kept on the window sill for that purpose. I so loved watching them through the window. Suddenly I saw a seagull swoop down, scattering the wrens, and carry off saucer and all. I screamed and dropped a cup into the sink, breaking it. Ever since that morning I have hated seagulls.

When I did nod off, it was even worse. A horrible, upsetting dream kept coming into my head. I dreamt I was a young woman again – thirtyish. I was standing on a very draughty street corner, clutching my handbag with one hand and holding my hat on with the other. Perhaps it was the seaside. It was too misty to see very far. Perhaps it was the wind from off the sea.

Suddenly, who should come round the corner but John, looking ever so young and handsome – just like in the photographs. He was holding the purse out in front of him, but this time it was properly gift-wrapped, with the most beautiful pink ribbon on top, tied in a bow. I don't know how I knew it was the purse inside. I just did. As he came up, I smiled and held out my hand for his gift, but he didn't give it to me. There was someone else standing just behind me – I never actually saw her face in the dream, but I knew she was there. I felt her presence somehow – and he handed it to her instead. He just smiled at me fleetingly and then gave it to her. He even kissed her on the cheek. I heard it – just behind my back. He'd ignored me – just like Harold in the rear-view mirror.

When I turned to look at them, they were already some distance away – at least a hundred yards. The wind carried their laughter back to me. They were walking in step, so jauntily that they might almost have been dancing. His arm was across her back, protecting her. Her head was resting against his shoulder.

Then I woke up. The birds had stopped singing by now – except the occasional mewing of a seagull. It was a cold, rainy day. I could hear it driving against the window panes. I got up to make myself a cup of tea. I felt giddy from lack of sleep, but – worse than that – I felt sore, bruised, jealous, as if he really had betrayed me. I hated myself for it because I knew full well that he was in hospital, and that he was the kindest and most caring man I had ever met in my life, the only one. I knew he would never have done such a thing to me – never ever.

As I was pouring out the tea, it dawned on me why I had dreamt about it, why I had imagined him giving it to somebody else. It was all Harold's fault. He'd put the idea into my head years ago. He'd picked it up at the reception and looked at it. I must have left it on the sideboard. I was less careful with it in those days. As soon as I saw that he had it in his hands, I went across to retrieve it. I didn't like the idea of him handling it. It made it seem slightly soiled. We didn't get on even then. I used to hate it when he invited John to the pub. They didn't go very often – perhaps once a month. Margaret and I never went with them. I don't think we were ever invited. Neither of us liked pubs very much anyway. They're such noisy, smoky places. John, being kindness itself, didn't have the heart to refuse. And he never got drunk or anything like that – just a little more outgoing. And his cheeks had a bit more colour in them. I quite liked the smell of beer on his breath, though I wouldn't drink it myself.

Anyway, I stepped over and asked for it back. Harold just pretended not to notice, not to hear. I think he'd had a little more champagne than anybody else. I asked again, a bit more forcefully.

I was quite angry by now. It was my property after all. He heard me this time. He plonked it into my hand, smiling down at it wryly.

He rarely looked you straight in the eye. I didn't like that about him either. His words weren't offensive in themselves. It was the way he said them, what he might have meant them to mean. What I took them to mean after I'd had a good think about them. 'Is it new?' he said. 'It's John's wedding gift,' I replied curtly, and turned my back on him. The times I've turned those words of his over in my mind. The times I've wondered to myself whether he knew more about John's past than I did, whether they'd ever talked about people I didn't know at the pub...

In a way I was glad I remembered his words just then because it meant that the dream – however silly – had at least come from somewhere. And that made me feel easier. I even became less anxious about the purse itself. Funnily enough, it turned up in the most unlikely of places a couple of weeks later. Harold found it under the driver's seat one Sunday when he was hoovering out the car. I must have dropped it on the way back from the hospital – or something. Margaret gave it back to me, told me to keep it in a safe place next time. The awful thing is I lost it again a couple of weeks later. By that time I'd had to buy another. John's purse wasn't really big enough to keep all the loose change in I needed for the hospital and back twice a day. There's nothing worse than loose change for pulling a purse out of shape, is there? And conductors tend to get so cross if you wave pound notes at them all the time.

David was the first to see the mess I'd made in the annex. I hadn't mentioned it to Margaret. I felt a bit foolish later, as though I'd let go of myself or something. I think it was Margaret who must have put him up to coming that first weekend. He would have known how upset I'd been, how much I'd been affected by his uncle's fall.

She would have told him everything. They talk almost every day.

They've always been very close. That's only to be expected of an only child. Even Harold thought the world of him – so he couldn't have been all bad. He is such a lovely boy is David, so innocent and considerate, so much like John in many ways... Very young for his age as well – he must be all of thirty-six or seven by now. How time does fly!

We sat next to each other in the back of the car last weekend. There was room enough for four – not counting the arm rests. Trust Harold to do things in style. It didn't surprise me. Margaret told me a long time ago he had money put by for his funeral. Six black limousines though! Six! Practically filled the street. I never knew he had so many friends. Funny that John and Harold should have died within a year of each other.

David leant over and saw the purse. I was clutching it in my hand. It was the first time I'd used it in years. Is it new? he asked. I laughed. I'd only given it a polish. It does polish up beautifully. I told him it was a present from John. John's wedding present. That old! he said and whistled. I let him have a look. He put it to his nose and sniffed. Then he opened it and saw the handkerchief. That was the only reason I'd taken it. He read the label. Italian, he said, smiling. I nodded.

It sounded so romantic when he said it. Then I suddenly thought of John carrying it all that way – just for me. Tramping along those dusty roads under the blazing Italian sun in his khaki shorts, whistling one of his tunes...

CUSTARD

Usually he just flew out the door, arm wings tipping left then right, belted twice round the back yard, nearly but not quite banging against the shed where papa kept his BSA, and then flew into the kitchen again with an almighty VROOOOOM. His mum would laugh fit to bursting. There's something not quite all there with you, me lad, what the devil's got into you, she'd say, gosterin away.

I'm a plane! he'd shout. An' I'm off again, watch out!

It weren't like that today though. Today he were rubbish, fit for nowt. He couldn't even walk about, let alone tek off. His head felt all thick and swimmy and peculiar.

Me head feels all thick and swimmy and peculiar, he told her. His voice felt small an all. He just didn't feel like bellowin. He couldn't even lift his head up off the pillow. It felt like a great heavy wet football. She'd had to come up to the bedroom to see what was what. No amount of calling could fetch him down to breakfast.

What's got into you then, laddo? she said, bustling in as she wiped her hands on her pinny. You're hot, you know. Your hair's wet through. It's all sticky. She kept running her hands through his hair. He kept his eyes closed because the light hurt a bit. It were like needles prickin. His eyelids felt heavy an' all. What are we gonna do with you then? she said. She looked right worried.

A glass of Lucozade and Custer's Last Stand, he said, with a bit of tragedy in his voice...

She wanted him downstairs where she could keep an eye on him, so he leant on her on the way down, pushing his legs out at every step. He felt as daft and as sloppy as a puppet.

I'm reyt peculiar today, mum, he said. I've got heavy

legs. I just don't know what's got into me. As if I didn't know, she said, supporting him as they walked down side by side. We don't want you fallin'... She had such a serious look on. She looked like she did when rent man came callin' on a Thursday. This were a Monday though. Flippin' football at school an all! Missin football!

She settled him on the sofa, with the yellow blanket over him, the scratchy one. Papa was already shakin the thermometer for all it was worth. Then he popped it in, under the tongue. It felt cold and slippery. Don't you let it slip out, little man.

He shook his head, slowly. It were a right effort even to do that. I shan't, he said, with teary eyes. He didn't want to be shouted at. He felt too weak to be shouted at.

Papa took it out. Way up, he said to mum, without looking back at him. Let him stop at home for a bit of cossetin.

He kept starin' into the glass of Lucozade on the chair next to the sofa. It were a funny orange colour. You drink it, mum said, it'll do you a world of good. He felt that drowsy when he looked at that glass. It were just as if he were swimmin' in it. Custer's Last Stand, his favourite book, were propped open next to his cushion, with that picture of him chargin' across the plains.

Papa's big face suddenly appeared in front of him, with a big yellow tin. Custer or Custard with your apple pie, laddo?

He grinned and jabbed at the tin.

BIG, BAD LAUGHTER

He couldn't say anything. He couldn't speak. The words were there, inside his head, but he couldn't get them out. He wanted to say: I don't want to. I don't want to go back there. You won't make me either. But he couldn't say it. He couldn't say anything.

He could hear them talking about him, faintly, as if the voices weren't quite there. They kept swimming in and out. It looked like they were underwater. The mouths were moving, very slowly, heads bending back and forth. Like fish underwater, coming very close to the camera, and then swimming away again.

He wanted to get up and go, just walk out, but his body didn't do anything. It just kept on sitting there, listening to what they were saying, listening without really hearing. His head felt thick and furry. Too heavy to hold it up, so he let it slump forward a bit. He was looking at his knees now, on the edge of the bed, lumpy, shiny knees. He pulled the white gown shut so that he couldn't see his knees.

WHAT DOES *HE* THINK THEN?

All of a sudden he heard that, in a great blast of sound. He looked up. He jerked his head up because he knew that he was the one being asked. He didn't know though, did he? He knew he didn't know what he thought. It was all mud now, thick mud from ear to ear. Once upon a time he'd known. All he knew was that he didn't want to go back. And he couldn't even say that. All he could do was open his mouth.

The doctor stood up, and walked up to him. He put his arm across his back. He rubbed it, round and round, pushing him forward. He mussed up his hair a bit. He smelt of cigarettes.

He's a very clever lad, this lad, he said, speaking to them on their chairs. He mustn't let it go to waste. If he goes back, he'll make something of himself. If he stays here, he'll be stuck in a rut. This is his big chance. He'll buck up. We're all a bit frightened of the big bad world.

Then he laughed so loud that the room shook, and everything fell to bits.

A DAY TO REMEMBER

On the evening of grandmother's laying out, and quite unknown to the rest of the family, Louis slipped out of the apartment where all the relations were gathered, and went down into the street, stealthy as a ghost.

The street seemed so strange. It was like a holiday out there. No one seemed to know or to care that grandmother had died, and so Louis told no one, not even his friend from the *boulangerie*.

Instead, he walked and walked until he reached the river. And there he stopped and looked, squeezed between two *bouquinistes*, who were too busy arranging and re-arranging their books and their cellophane-wrapped engravings to pay any attention to one small boy in stiff grey clothes.

At this time of year, there were usually lots of pleasure steamers carrying visitors up and down the river, and when Louis had been a very tiny boy, almost too tiny to walk very properly, he remembered, his grandmother would bring him to see the people gliding by on the water in their flouncy, colourful clothes. He would wave at them and they would wave back. Sometimes the gentlemen would even raise their slender canes at him, and grandmother would tell him to smile a proper smile because he in particular would be what they remembered best about Paris. And that he thought strange. His grandmother had been a little strange – but quite lovely as well.

But today there was nothing down there, not even a solitary rowing boat. And the river itself looked so grey and so still that Louis imagined that it might have stopped flowing altogether.

Suddenly, Louis heard what he took for a long, low

blast on a trumpet, but no matter in which direction he looked, he couldn't seem to see where it had come from. But when he turned round to peer down at the river again, something quite extraordinary had happened, and in the blink of an eye.

A great black funeral barge was now moored directly beneath him on the river. Louis could see the magnificent coffin quite clearly, raised up high on a gold plinth in the middle of the boat, gorgeously draped in the flag of the French Republic.

It reminded Louis of Napoleon's coffin in the Invalides, the one that his grandmother had taken him to see. Yes, it was certainly as big as that one. And standing on the deck were hundreds – it certainly seemed that many – of mourners, in their long black tail coats and top hats, many with medals pinned to their chests, rows of them, and blue sashes around their waists. But there was no sunlight to make those medals winks back at him.

Who has died? thought Louis. What important person has died without my even hearing of it? Could it be the President himself?

Back at the apartment of the deceased, Great-Uncle Marcel had just happened to notice that Louis was missing. Another boy – some cousin or other that very few of the assembled party were even able to put a name to – had asked after him, and a quick search in the four dark, meagre rooms of the apartment had revealed his absence – to the mingled horror and consternation of his mother, the deceased's daughter, who was generally known to suffer from a feeble heart and various other related complaints.

'It cannot be!' she muttered, falling back heavily into a rather fragile cane chair that had been bequeathed to her. 'It cannot be that my only boy has gone too!'

Suddenly, Louis felt someone behind him, pushing, even kicking him a little. He looked round, and to his astonishment he saw that the *quai* was now crowded with people wearing long black coats and black dresses – but not quite of a splendour to match those people on the boat. It was a little child in a black, lacy bonnet who had kicked him. It was being held in its mother's arms, up painfully high so that it could see what was happening down there on the river...

The next thing that Louis heard was the tramp, tramp, tramp of feet somewhere down below. He strained up on his tiptoes so that he could catch a glimpse of the broad path that ran beside the river.

Yes, there were soldiers down there, marching in solemn step, eight in a row, with yet another soldier at the front, out ahead on his own, holding a baton of sorts across his chest – sideways. He was almost certainly the leader, Louis could see that from the tremendously important expression on his face and the great plumed helmet that he was wearing.

Then they stopped, all of them, all at once, and the soldier at the front jerked his baton up into the air. At that signal, almost as if they were puppets that were being manipulated by some puppeteer like the one who had entertained Louis and his five special friends at his last birthday party, all the soldiers swivelled their heads upwards and sideways so that they were looking directly at the gleaming coffin on which that beautiful French flag was now stirring a little in the chilly breeze.

Louis' mother was still rushing from room to room, but everyone barring her had given up hope of finding him by now. Great-Uncle Marcel caught her as she flew throughthe parlour once again, and held her sobbing against his chest.

'Don't be surprised, my little one,' he said, stroking her hair, something that he had not done since she was a little child in his arms. How coarse and brittle it felt now! 'He has probably slipped off to enjoy himself. It is too much for children, all this business...'

He did not like to mention the death of his sister

directly because that would be to criticise Louis somewhat for skipping off in the way that he had done. 'He is a good boy at heart, and he is old enough to look after himself.' It is all true, he thought, looking down at his niece's trembling hand. She is distraught because her mother has died. She is acting quite unreasonably. Her good sense will prevail by and by. Time heals all things.

Upstairs in grandmother's bedroom, the priest was busy laying a thin film of white gauze over the old woman's chest, abdomen and legs, now thin as a sparrow's, to make her look serenely beautiful. After all, any moment now they would all come trooping in again to pay their last respects to her. Suddenly, he spotted the pesky little fly that had settled on the wart on the tip of her nose end. That will most certainly not do, he said to himself, whipping a clean handkerchief out of the pocket of his *soutane* and giving the creature a hefty swipe. Like all flies everywhere, it skipped off, and then hung about that room's sombre, heavy drapes, waiting for its next heaven-sent opportunity.

When the band had begun to play its slow, solemn march, Louis saw his chance. The crowd had begun to thin out by now – he could even hear snatches of laughter – and a gap had appeared that would enable him to reach the top of the steps that led straight down to the edge of the river itself...

Louis was so desperate to go down there and find out what was happening, who it was exactly that had died. He had enquired of several people, including the mother of the child who had been kicking him in the back, but she had been so choked up with tears that she had not been able to answer him. So Louis must find out for himself – as long as *they* would let him, of course, because even as he reached the top of the long flight of stone steps, Louis could see the soldiers standing at the bottom, two abreast, with their backs to him, legs spread, blocking his way.

Louis crept down all the same, while every minute

expecting to hear a whistle or a voice shouting to him that he must go away immediately – or be clapped into prison. But no, it did not come. Everyone continued to stare directly at the great barge itself, even though the people on deck, all those dignitaries, were no longer standing still, but milling about and even chatting to each other. Two of them were blowing cigarette smoke into the air. It was as if they have been woken up from a sleep, Louis thought to himself.

'Excuse me,' Louis said to the taller of the two soldiers closest to him, 'may I pass by?' It seemed from the look he gave him that the soldier simply could not believe his eyes. The bare-faced cheek, the audacity of the little fellow! his eyes seemed to say. But there was also just a touch of kindness in them, and that is why I must at least *try*, Louis was thinking to himself as he began to walk, slowly and calmly, towards the gang plank of the great barge itself...

Four, five steps... The gang plank trembled a little as Louis walked up it, but still no one tried to stop him. He could not believe his luck. It seemed like a kind of miracle... And then he thought that perhaps it *was* a miracle after all. Yes, perhaps, after all, he was invisible...

But no, because now, at the top of the gangplank, stood a small boy not much bigger than himself, and Louis knew that the boy had seen him because he was smiling and beckoning. And yet how different they looked, these two, in other respects: Louis, so plain and homespun in his old grey suit with its little black corduroy collar and cuffs, and this other one in his black top hat and tail coat! Louis had never imagined that they made clothes like that for small children. He thought that only the grandest of adults wore them – great ambassadors and such like – on their famous state occasions.

Now Louis and the other boy were standing face to face, and Louis could see that his friend – already he thought of him like that, which was very strange because Louis did not make friends with other boys very easily, being so shy and inward-looking – had been crying because his cheeks and all around his eyes looked smeary and smudgy from all the tears that he must have wiped away...

The boy held out his hand and Louis took it without any hesitation.

'My grandmother has died,' said the boy. 'Won't you come and meet my father?'

Louis held back, more than a little apprehensive now. Should he proceed – or just turn tail and run away? Could it really be true that *both* their grandmothers had died – or was he just dreaming it?

But when the boy squeezed Louis' hand, and smiled at him with such warmth in his eyes, Louis felt a little calmer, and he let himself be drawn into and through the crowd – though he hardly dared to raise his eyes for fear of meeting some mocking or superclious glance. After all, what right had he, looking as he did and being who he was, to be amongst all these people? Louis comforted himself by thinking that his grandmother would have understood his feelings. She too had felt very awkward in the company of people she thought better – or, at least – grander, than herself.

When Louis' mother looked down for the last time into her own mother's pale, frozen face, she thought to herself – with precious little emotion; in fact, so little as to surprise even her – it is not she who is there now. She has gone away. But where to? For, deep inside herself, she did not believe that her mother had gone directly to Paradise – or was even on her way there – in spite of the presence of Father Lefèbvre in the room, and the way that he had glanced across at her, and then stared into her eyes, almost as if he were divining that everything was not quite as it should be inside her. But she had grown accustomed to concealing her lack of faith over a period of many years, and so it had not been too difficult for her to smile back at him quite warmly and unaffectedly. And that smile had seemed to satisfy him.

'We should remember her as she was,' he was saying, and it was more like the low, muffled buzzing of a somnolent fly, the sound of his voice on the air, and not words with real meaning at all. And that is why, she thought to herself later, as she drifted from the room at the head of the relatives, almost as if it were a solemn procession down the nave of a church, that is why I paid so little heed to his words. And yet, in spite of her lack of faith, she could not all the same bring herself to admit, not at that moment anyway, that she found him a rather tiresome old man, who uttered, more often than not, the most wearisome banalities: 'We should remember her as she was, and give thanks for her gentle piety in the most straitening of life's circumstances...' They had floated upon the air, those words, like the small, marvellously delicate head of some cherub upon a goose-down pillow...

Louis's new friend was hitting the back of an enormous man who was standing with others like him in a circle, sipping from a long-stemmed glass. Louis flinched at every blow.

'Papa! Papa! Look!'

When Papa had quite finished talking and drinking for the moment, he wiped his small, pink mouth briskly on a white handkerchief and then, very slowly, turned in their direction – as if it was quite difficult for him to move at all. Or as if, Louis was thinking to himself, he is himself some great boat on the river that is making a long, slow turn to the accompaniment of hoots and whistles, before it goes back in the direction from which it has come...

The first thing that Louis noticed was the huge brush of a moustache that seemed to conceal his nostrils almost entirely; and the darkness of his eyes, whose colour alone looked immediately threatening to Louis.

'And what have we here?' he said in a rumbling,

thundery sort of voice as he bent forward very stiffly from the waist. This action caused some of the many medals that he was wearing to hang away from his clothes like so many bells...

'I have invited him, Papa...' said Louis' new friend with great eagerness, as if the presence of Louis beside him were one of the most exciting events of his life.

'So *you* have invited *him*?' repeated the Papa, who was examining Louis all over with his great black eyes as if he had never before in his life seen something quite so strange. 'And what is the name of this person that you have invited – if he does indeed have a name?'

Louis tried to swallow, but his throat felt so dry and so papery that he could scarcely manage it. He had to say something though because his friend – and his friend's Papa – were staring and staring at him in such wonderment.

Louis' mother tore through the outer door of the apartment, clattered down the dim, curving stairwell, and swung out of the front door of the building, holding her black hat with its voluminous back crepe veil very firmly to her head, it being new and quite desirable in its own right once the veil were removed after the due passage of time. 'My darling, darling little Louis...,' she was muttering over to herself like a litany as she weaved this way and that along the pavement to avoid all the passers by, every one of whom seemed to be encumbered with boxes or parcels or market produce of one kind or another – merely to spite *me* for being in such a tearing hurry, she would have been inclined to tell herself, had she not known that such a thought was the most utter nonsense.

If only that foolish man had not insisted that we say our farewells to dear Maman just then though! she cursed. She was sure – absolutely certain, in fact – that it was not at all for the reason that he, Lefèbvre, had given: that by a quarter of five he must be away (on a wing and a prayer!) to visit yet another of those terminally sick in which his cosy little *quartier* seemed to abound this spring. 'And why spring?' he had added, raising his shoulders in a gesture of pious hopelessness. 'Is not spring a time of abundance? Surely autumn and winter are the seasons of death!'

She had not bothered to give even so much as a second's thought to such a foolish paradox because she knew very well where his footsteps would be taking him once he had departed: into the company of his fellow drinkers in that little bar on the rue Véron, where he had been known, according to one of her neighbours, to spend whole days at a time contemplating the remorseless passage of the hours...

Louis could not quite believe that it was he, Louis, who was riding in such a splendid carriage. It was like a dream from which he had still not awoken. Papa had been most kind to him after all. He had expressed deep regrets when Louis had explained that *his grand-mère* too had died, though not a great person like the *grand-mère* of – . He had indicated his little friend, who had said, very quickly, and eagerly, as if sensing Louis' embarrassment: 'Marcel! You must call me Marcel!'

Yes, Papa had expressed his most profound regrets, but then, almost immediately, he had said to him: 'We have a little procession through the streets of Paris in a few moments. Would you like to join us in the carriage? Marcel will look after you, won't you, my dear boy?' 'Of course, of course!' Marcel had said, making a sudden high jump that had dislodged his hat.

And so Louis was now riding in the carriage at the very front of the procession, staring out at all the people who were peering in at them with such an eager curiosity. It had seemed such a long journey back from the river. First, having crossed by the Pont Alexandre III, they had ascended the Champs Elysées with great dignity, and from there had made a wide circle around the Arc de Triomphe, before proceeding eastward along the *grands boulevards*, and always at such a stately and measured pace. And everywhere there had been the milling crowds of people, some rich, some poor, depending upon which *quartier* they were passing through.

Louis had loved every minute of it. And one of his private reasons for loving it so much was that he knew just how much his dear dead *grand-mère* would have loved it too, she who had looked after him all his life, his mother being such a poor, sickly woman, forever taking herself off to sanitoria in the company of doctors and fussy female helpers... She had been such a kind, curious old lady, so ready to marvel at the marvellous world of Paris, even though she and Louis had lived in the most modest of circumstances in the eighteenth *arrondissement*...

And now what — in the name of the creator — have I got myself entangled with! fumed Louis' mother as she tried to cross the seething boulevard. Goodness me, what a time and a place for a funeral procession! But it was quite impossible. The gendarme would allow no one through and, truth to tell, apart from her, no one seemed to be inclined to cross and to walk on anyway. They were all gazing awestruck as the gleaming black carriages passed on their way, and remarking upon how the horses were behaving with such discipline — even the very horses. Not once had they seen a whip come down on a gleaming flank, not once!

And it was all the worse for her, of course, because she was not even tall enough to see properly what was going on. That would, at least, have been some small compensation for such an infuriating impediment to her progress...

At last — at last! — a tall, youngish man whose eye she happened to catch — she was not at all bad-looking, for all that she was now forty-one years of age and afflicted with so many complaints, she reminded herself as she returned his glance just a touch coquettishly, but not too much because she had noticed immediately that his clothes were not of the finest kind – stood aside and beckoned her forward...

And it was at that moment precisely that she thought she saw someone, a child like hers, uncannily so, in a carriage at the very front of the procession which was now receding from view so quickly that even as she thought she had recognised his quick turning face, and even his arm as it rose in a cheerful wave, she knew, in her heart of hearts, that it could not, of course, possibly be him, her own dearest darling Louis. It was just – yet again – one of life's bitter little illusions.

Which was why, in part, she accepted the invitation from the young man to take a little *apéro* with him, in order to steady her nerves. In order to prepare herself for the worse that was to come. In order, perhaps, even to divert herself from it all for a few fleeting moments of questionable happiness – even were they to happen at all! – in the trembling arms of some passing stranger.

DETACHMENT

John Gilbert came across the head one sultry Saturday afternoon in mid-to-late September when he was busy pruning his little garden hedge with the big pruning shears, knocking it about for all he was worth. In fact, he almost stumbled over the stupid thing, giving his ankle a nasty twist for what would have been the second time in two months.

He nudged it with the side of his foot, a little gingerly at first, wondering to himself how it got there. Then he picked it up in both hands and turned it full circle to get a better idea of it. It wasn't old by any means – and by that he meant not long parted from the body. All the flesh was still intact, the eyes and so forth. The complexion looked healthy enough. It wasn't all that big either now her came to give it a good, hard look, more the head of a child than a grown up. But what child? He hadn't heard of a child losing its head lately. There'd been no tales of missing heads, big or small, in the village that week.

So he took it indoors, and put it down on the mantelpiece between the alarm clock and the marble egg they'd been given for Christmas, that daft marble egg that was no good to anybody. What was the sense in a marble egg?

And, having popped it up there, and sat himself down in his favourite armchair, he picked up his newspaper, placed it over his face, and promptly fell asleep. John Gilbert had never had any trouble falling asleep, night or day, and his wife (bless her soul) said it was because he'd never had a care in the world. He'd nodded when she'd said that, supposing she was right.

It was not long though before he got a rude awakening – thanks to his daughter, who'd come running in for her tea, all hot and thirsty from her playing, and seen the head sitting there on the mantelpiece. She screamed so loud that John Gilbert nearly fell out of his chair from the shock of it.

'What ever is the matter with you, Julie?' he said. 'Can't you see your old father's trying to get forty winks of sleep?'

But all she did was to point up at it, and her small hand was trembling like a leaf. So he got up from his chair, took her up in his arms, and let her sob a bit into his shoulder, turning her round and round the floor as if they were doing a spot of dancing together because he knew how she liked that. He always did that when she was upset, and most times it worked a treat. Not this time though. Oh no. This time she just screamed and screamed, and the noise almost drove him barmy. But he saw it was no good shouting back at her or slapping the backs of her legs like he'd done other times when she wouldn't for the life of her stop being a naughty child. No, this time he tried reasoning with her a little, saying soft, soothing words to win her round.

'There, there, Julie,' he said, 'it's only a head when all's said and done. It's not about to hurt you or anything, is it? How can it hurt you? Why, it hasn't even got legs to run with. The only thing it could do is bite with its teeth, and how can it even do that when it doesn't have a body to carry it about?'

But she screamed all the louder when he said that, and took a great bite out of John Gilbert's shoulder. And that made him really mad. He flung her onto the sofa and knelt down beside her, but instead of looking back at him, she pushed her face into a cushion.

And still she was sobbing and sobbing as if her little heart would burst open. So he tried a slightly different tack.

'Do you know the head then, Julie?' he said. 'Do you know who it belongs to by any chance, girl?'

And at that she let out another piercing scream, a

scream so deafening that it almost burst John Gilbert's sensitive ear drum, the left one, so he didn't wait for an answer. He just plucked her up from the sofa, cushion and all, whisked her straight into her bedroom, threw her onto the unmade bed, and left her there, still sobbing, being careful to check that her windows were shut fast so that her weeping and wailing wouldn't bring all those nebby neighbours running. Then he stepped out of her bedroom, turned the key in the lock, and slipped it into the pocket of his black waistcoat. Best to let her sleep it off, he was thinking to himself. Sometimes she goes a bit too far for her own good, that girl...

John Gilbert glanced down at his own hand, and he saw that one was trembling too, and he hated to see it. There was nothing he liked more than a bit of peace and a quiet heart, and nothing he detested quite so much as shouting and screaming and kicking up a terrible commotion. And so he lay flat out on the sofa to calm himself, across the very spot where she had lain a moment or two ago, and settled down to staring at the head.

He stared and stared at it, daring it to stare back at him, but he knew it couldn't. It was just a head, that's all, just a head without a body, and heads don't work without bodies, he knew that right enough. Hadn't he said it over to himself again and again? But still he stared, he couldn't seem to stop himself staring. It was almost as if he was taunting it, daring it to look in his direction. But it never looked. How could it? And at that he smiled a broad smile, a broad, happy smile. Then he stood up on his big legs, marched across to the fireplace, and gave it a great big cuff across the side of the face so that it fell onto the floor and came to rest behind the chair. He leant over the arm and gently picked it up again, cradling it in both his hands, and placed it back beside the clock in its old place. And it wasn't too much damaged, just a little bruising to the left cheek directly below the eye, and a smut or two in the eye itself, perhaps a spot of coal dust, but that didn't matter much either because the eye wasn't working any more, was it? It was just a pretend eye now, wasn't it? Of course it was...

And with that he stretched himself on the sofa again to try and snatch those forty odd winks of sleep she's cheated him of, that girl of his, just a little while ago, and he yawned a great big noisy yawn, closed up the heavy lids of his eyes, and was off and away before you could say Jack Robinson.

It was that persistent hammering on the door that woke him up with a start – for the second time that day! He sat up in the dark and looked about. There was a little light in that room – just enough to see by, there being more than a sliver of moon in the sky that night, but the very fact that he'd slept so long and woken up in a dark room, albeit his own, instead of a light one, set his heart racing inside his waistcoat, and his brain feverishly wondering whoever that could be hammering like that at this time of night... And there it was again, that pounding on the door.

But which door? He couldn't rightly tell in the dark, for all that he was twitching his head about like a nervy chicken. Could it be *her* door, he wondered, glowering at it... And then he heard the voice, that neighbour's voice, calling from the kitchen, and he practically threw himself across the room to the kitchen door once he knew she'd stepped into the house, because he hated them stepping inside his little castle, those neighbours of his, he hated it even more than when they came skulking into his garden, peering and poking here and there for balls that had strayed and such like – or so they said. And even before he got his hand to the handle of that door, he shouted out in that great, booming voice of his:

'What is it you want?'

And directly he yanked it open, there she was, standing right behind it, the little woman from the house next door, grinning up at him through her gappy teeth, with her hands folded one on top of the other.

'So you're in, Mr Gilbert?' she said, meek as a lamb, and he thought to himself: of course I'm in! What does she think is standing here in front of her? The ghost of John Gilbert or what? Then he said it all over again, wanting to get her out just as quickly as he could because the electric light was blazing away in that kitchen, wasting all its precious juice, and she was the one who must have put it on in the first place. None other could have done it...

So she told him.

'You left your shears out of doors, your pruning shears, and it's coming on to rain, so I brought them indoors for you...'

She pointed to them, lying there askew on the bread board, but he wasn't quick to say his thanks. He didn't even remember leaving them out there. Perhaps it was just something she'd *thought* to say, some crafty excuse for poking around his house... So he just nodded, flung open the outer door – and felt the rain blow into his face. That bit of it is true anyway, he thought to himself, as he watched her hurrying back down the path with the shopping basket over her head, thinking also what a silly fool she looked.

Then he closed it again and locked it – and bolted it top and bottom for good measure. And he peeped out of the window too just to check that he couldn't glimpse a shadow of her flitting back up the lawn.

He stepped back into the living room and snapped on the light. Good god! It was a quarter to ten already by the clock on the mantelpiece, and he hadn't even fried up the liver and bacon for his tea yet – nor for hers neither...

And thinking of her again made him feel cold and unhappy inside himself. What could be the matter with that girl? She just wasn't the same since her mother went. It was only one day in three that she even spoke to him. Other times she slipped out of doors before he was awake, and took herself off to her bed before he came back from his work. What was the good of a daughter that couldn't give her own father a spot of company of an evening? Was she sick in the head or something?

He clawed up a slippery handful of the most delicious pig's liver from the old brown basin, tossed it into the frying pan with umpteen rashers of bacon, and watched it sizzling away to its heart's content. A few minutes later, having poked it about a bit with his fork, and hummed a couple of his favourite tunes to while away the time, he heaped it onto the plates, his and hers, beside the hob – three rashers for him and one for her and so on and so forth... Then, blowing on the plates for his finger ends' sake, he carried them back into the living room, still humming to himself, and wondered where they should sit on an exceedingly chilly night such as this one.

The card table! He picked up the little table from its place in the corner where it lay propped against the wall, and set it up in front of the fire so that they'd get the benefit of the heat from the dying embers. Then he laid the plates down – gently does it – on the green baize top of the table, one on one side of the clock, directly beneath that marble egg, and one on the other, underneath the head.

The smell of good food was pricking at his nostrils, so he ran across to her bedroom door, whipped the key out of his pocket, and poked it into the key hole. One quick twist of the wrist, the door was thrown back, and he strode, grimly smiling, into her room.

'Food's all ready for the eating, Julie,' he said, 'it's liver and bacon tonight, your favourite!'

To tell the gospel truth, liver and bacon was *his* especial favourite, but he knew that Julie would never refuse a plateful – especially as there was nothing else in the house.

He stared down at the small hump in the bed, the hump that he knew was his daughter, and waited for it to stir. But it did not stir. All it did was to rise and fall, regular as clockwork, so he guessed that meant she was still asleep and he hadn't shouted loud enough.

So he bent over her, and his mouth was not two inches from her her now, though he couldn't see it because she'd wrapped herself up from top to toe in the blanket like some stinking old mummy in its grave clothes. Not even a carroty sprig of her ginger hair was showing at the top. Yes, he bent right over her, practically double, and bellowed the words into her ear:

'It's ready, the food! It's piping hot now – but it'll soon be cold as Christmas!'

And with that the bundle shivered and began to sit up, clawing its hands out of all that wrapping. Up, up it came. None too quickly though, like a worm lifting its wavering head. Then, all of a sudden, the blankets fell away from the pale face and the blinking eyes, and the tousled, spiky hair.

As soon as he saw the hand come groping out, he gripped it in his own, and practically dragged her out of that bed because there was such a gnawing hunger in the pit of his stomach that they just had to make haste and be done with all this tomfoolery of stretching and yawning that the girl, he knew from of old, was so good at the best of times. And when she was off the bed and up on her legs, he bundled her out ahead of him, out of that darkened room and into the light and the sight of those plates of food, heaped up and steaming, that made his mouth run with spittle just to see them there. Why, he could have polished off the two of them together in the blink of an eye, but he couldn't let her go hungry, could he, not his very own daughter... Of course he couldn't.

Still holding her firmly by the arm, he pushed her round to the far side of the table, plopped himself down in his seat, and bade her sit down in hers. But she wouldn't sit down. She just stood beside the chair and stared at the head again, the head that was balanced directly over her plate, doing nothing but mind its own business. He had meant to put her in that seat, of course. It was all part of his little plan to get her used to seeing the thing, to get her over these silly tantrums. But as soon as she saw it, she began to whimper again, so he growled the words at her like a bear, and stabbed his finger in the direction of the empty chair.

'Sit you down now and eat!' he said, and she dragged herself into her seat, but instead of eating, her head fell forward onto her folded arms, and her shoulders started to twitch and jerk about all over again. But at least she was silent now, and not crying out loud any more, which meant he could eat his own plate of food in peace and quiet. Twice he spoke her name between mouthfuls, but neither time did she answer, so he settled down to doing nothing but eat and enjoy his own – and be damned to that plate of hers if she hadn't the gumption to take what was good for her...

And when his own plate was licked clean as a whistle, he saw that she still hadn't touched hers, not even one mouthful, so he pushed her head to one side and lifted it out of her reach. She must be taught a lesson, this one, he was thinking to himself, that if she does not eat the food she's given, another will happily eat it. She is not the only one to be hungry in this world. And with that he polished off her own plateful as well, but this one wasn't as satisfying as his own, not being quite so big.

He dropped the plates with a clatter, one on top of the other, wiped his greasy lips on the thick hairs of his forearm, sat back in his seat, and rubbed the fullness of his stomach with a smooth, circular motion. It felt as round and swollen as a football... Then he raised his eyes to her again.

Still she hadn't budged, but now he wasn't so cross with her any more, not now that he'd eaten his fill. A little patience had come creeping back from goodness knows where – and his old father's heart went out to her. So he spoke to her, quietly this time, hardly breathing the words, so that she wouldn't be frightened off by the sound of his voice.

'Julie,' he whispered, 'what you weeping for now? When

you going to stop all that weeping? It does you no good, you know. If your eyes are all dirty and puffed up, they won't have you at the Sunday School. They don't like to see blubbering at the Sunday School. Sunday School is for happy children...'

And she heard him. He knew that she heard him because *he* heard the gulp-gulp in her throat as she swallowed the saliva, and he saw the sharp bone of her Adam's apple move up and down, stretching the smooth flesh of her throat... That meant she was getting ready to speak, so he waited, biting his lip, to see what she'd say.

She raised her head and looked straight at him through the thin slits of her eyes, and the sight of that face was just as he had said: all smeary and dirty like an unwashed kitchen floor. But he smiled at her all the same, a loving smile, and put out a hand to her across the table, beckoning with his ring finger, half-hoping that she might even slip out of her seat and come and sit herself down on his knee. And then he would have cradled her in his hands and sung a little song into her ear, and even bounced her up and down on his knee just as if she'd been a tiny babe again and not the boisterous ten-year-old she'd so quickly grown into while his back was turned – at least, that's how it seemed.

'Well....?' he said, having bided his time for an answer, 'tell me what it is that's in that head of yours...'

She went to move her lips, and no sound came out barring the tiniest croak, and now the lower one was quivering. Then it came.

'I don't like it...' was all that she said, squeezing out the words, half turning her head towards it again, but hardly daring to look.

'What!' he snapped, standing and kicking his chair back from the table. 'You don't like it, you say? But there's nothing there, Julie. It's just a head now. Go on, touch it and see.'

And with one quick step he was standing beside her

and, gripping her wrist, he was pushing her fingers at it. But she pulled back for all she was worth. She wouldn't, she couldn't, she just could not abide to touch it. My god, she is strong, this one, he marvelled, pulling her against him, but not a quarter as strong as me...

He pushed her fingers towards it quite smoothly and slowly so that it shouldn't happen too quickly. Now her finger, the smallest, was touching the eyeball, just brushing the fleck of smut on the white of the eyeball, but she wasn't looking, she was still fighting to stop it, that touching.

And now she was throwing her body about with such fury, the only thing he could do was to wind his arms right round her chest and squeeze, squeeze her up tight against him, squeezing the breath from her body, just to stay all that fury of shuddering and pulling and shaking and squirming. And he bellowed:

'Be still! Won't you be still, and just look at him, look at him now that he's quiet, obedient, not forever thrusting his tongue out at me!'

Then he let go of her, dropping her, all of a sudden, pushing her aside, and stood back, thinking to himself: Well I never, happen I'm right! Happen it was the one that stuck his tongue out at me every end and turn after all!

It was like a clap of thunder, the way that sneaky old devil of a thought had sprung into his head.

LOSING HIM

In my imagination, it sloped directly down to the sea from the window, a smooth gradient of pebbles, a matter of a few feet only. And how marvellous it was to dip your toe in the water first thing in the morning!

He would go before me – he was always in so much of a hurry. No sooner awake than he was running, running, running, never still for a single moment. I liked that. He never stopped going until he stopped for good.

It was a modest enough place – four wooden walls, a single bedroom, an ancient hob to cook on, to warm your hands at. And a little bit of outside space too, front and back. At the back, a snatch of garden where couch grass, a poppy or two, and a few hardy thistles grew. Of the front, you already know.

But it was our place. It was entirely sufficient because we cleaved to each other like the two hinged parts of a closed shell. It was only a matter of time, I suppose, before we got prised open. Foolish of us to think otherwise.

What did we do all day? We read. We talked. We made a little music with our voices, which did not sound too bad together. Quite harmonious in fact. *Barbara Allen*, when we sang it in unison, brought tears to our eyes. It made us clasp hands all the harder. We always stood to sing it, side on to the window.

What were we running from? We never spoke about it. We never told each other. A chance meeting at a pub, his offer of a quiet drink in the corner, and we were together, pledged to each other. That's how it felt, though neither of us ever said. There were the odd signs, of course – that strange long, deep scar across the back of his hand, as if someone had dragged something sharp and painful across it. I used to stroke it. My fingers travelled up and down the groove of it when we lay in bed, side by side, thigh pressed to thigh. It felt strangely comforting to both of us, we both said that, for me to be stroking it like that, quietly, steadily, wordlessly...

There were so few words between us! You could scarcely credit such an absence of conversation! But that is exactly how we liked it. I come from a family of big talkers, endless talkers. I grew sick of it. I became wedded to silence at a very young age. I would take myself off first thing in the morning, sit in the lavvy, in order to be engulfed by the sweetness of silence, all those useless words falling away. He was much the same. A little humming satisfied him. Perhaps there was not much to be told. I doubt it though. I think we were both closing a door on ourselves, and all to the good, in our opinion. Silence can be so healing.

What was it exactly that got him so agitated? It never made much sense to me. One day he was about his usual business – a morning run beside the sea, a little business, he said, in the hotel up the road. I never asked him what business. It was when he came back that the man had changed. There was a new look of alertness about him, like a bird looking out, anxiously, for its young. Was it for me? Perhaps not. He was switching his head from side to side, as if listening out for something. Opening and closing his mouth. Hard-swallowing. I took his hand, gripped it hard, gave him a look of puzzlement. He slipped his hand out of mine, stripped himself naked, and ran out the back door and down the pebbles. He plunged in, and began to swim, so furiously, as if he knew exactly where he was heading. I followed him with my eyes until I lost him.

THE BECHSTEIN ROOM

Unsurprisingly, the closure of the Bechstein Room seemed to make very little difference. One week we were all crowded in there, queueing for our sherry, our orange juice or our coffee (not more than one of the three, and given in exchange for the surrender of one's concert ticket), and then we were out. The door was closed. Locked. I even turned the handle that day, furtively, glancing back before I did so. That's how I knew. It was almost a child's prank. Oh, the little tricks learnt at one end of a long life...

We made a joke of it, of course. That was our way. Were we here for the music or the humour? (Always understated, needless to say.) Both, I don't doubt it for a moment. At first, of course, it was the ritual which had seduced us. The silence. The red velvet seats. The anticipation of a secular epiphany. We were runaways, both of us, renegades, from god. One god. Many gods. If not god, why not music? Both of us had asked that very same question of ourselves, it seems, one Sunday morning, you in a small flat just around the corner, I in a rattly house in Streatham. Slow mornings? Mornings of yawning emptiness? Mornings of a single boiled egg, pertly upright in its egg cup, centred on a plate, with a light strewing of toast dancing in attendance? Perhaps. Not necessarily. For whatever reason, we had both reached the same conclusion. Music on a Sunday morning, no matter what the season, is less contentious, more soothing, altogether. There is spirituality hiding in the spryness of Mozart at 11.30...

We had never sat together in the auditorium. There could be no planning, not for me anyway. I was a chancer, an early *arriviste*, looking out for a return when the hall has been declared, officially, full. All the excitement of the late capture. And I was always lucky. The absent god smiled down on me. If not in the auditorium then, where did we meet? We happened upon each other, seated on contiguous chairs, in those long minutes of lovely aftermath, when we all went downstairs, a great surge, like Pharaoh's tribes untroubled by the tides, into the Bechstein Room, thirsting for what was included in the price of a single ticket. Such a lovely idea.

I always opted for the orange juice, you for the coffee. Too much coffee jangles the nerves. You hated the chill of orange juice in the mouth, the throat, its pitiless flow. I felt it to be cleansing. We said these things to each other, eventually, not quite casually, from our contiguous chairs, gilded, which were set in a line. Nothing comes easily, at a certain age. Nothing feels impromptu any more. Everything is so well rehearsed, like the music we listened to there. We savour the exquisite predictability of it all, the way it sets the world to rights, momentarily, the way it sets us walking in a straight line when we might otherwise be inclined to meander, dangerously.

You struck up first. I had not even noticed you. I was staring down into the near weightless emptiness of a styrofoam cup – my mouth felt just cool enough, palate well cleansed – thinking about the pleasure we had both taken, Brahms and Mozart, in what we had just heard, those two string quintets, in F and C respectively. Brahms was always so hard to satisfy, page after page of score thrown to the floor in sheer exasperation. Until this, his String Quintet in F, Opus 88, written in 1882. It was as close to perfect as he could ever make it, he had declared. How happy I felt for him. It was just then that you said it.

Will it ever be open again? you asked, with a touch of mock-mournfulness in your voice, as if you were rehearsing the part of some great tragedian. *It doesn't feel quite right, to be here and not there...* I heard the words. I looked up. I twisted my body towards you – an ancient neck problem. Were they for me, those words? You were smiling, steadily, patiently, as if not quite knowing whether I had heard them at all, readying yourself, at a second's notice, to try again...

Mystery wrapped in mystery, I replied, introducing myself with a grave, outstretched hand. Robert. Muriel. Then we paused, wondering how to proceed. You poured words into the breech. I listened and smiled. Your voice was light, your words spoken with a hurried passion. The concert. Brahms. A touch of autobiography.

It all seems so long ago.

We walked out together. Pleasingly mild for a mid-October noon. The balm of warming sunlight on the cheek. When we reached the corner of Wimpole Street, you said: I go left here. I saluted you. I even clicked my heels. That struck me, later, as gauche, inappropriate, and even a touch ridiculous.

On the following Sunday, I found myself looking out for you. My eyes strayed around, somewhat purposelessly. Needless to say, the Bechstein Room was still closed. I drank my orange juice rather quickly. I felt harried, dissatisfied, for no particular reason. Could you have been the reason? I felt a pressing need to leave, to be gone from there. The Estonian violinist had been a touch on the arrogant side. Believing himself to be a great virtuoso, he had done three encores. How we had all hurried downstairs when the door closed on him for the final time, to the thinnest trickle of applause!

Three weeks later, by which time I had settled in to a belief that you would not return for reasons wholly inexplicable, you were standing in front of me in the queue for orange juice. Orange juice! You had not seen me. I stalked you. You were swaying a little as you walked. I got up close before I spoke. Not orange juice, Muriel! My goodness, what a change of heart! You turned. I got the shock of my life.

There was purple bruising over your left brow, a long arc. The entire eye socket looked a little swollen and tender. Your eye was bloodshot. Oh dear! I said. You told me what had happened as we walked over to our seats. You had fallen on the step up from the pavement. It had been a nasty business. You had lost consciousness. It was your first time out since the accident. The paramedics had been wonderful, really, truly wonderful. You had chosen orange juice because of its soothingness, you told me, delicately indicating your mouth. Had that been damaged too then? You didn't explain.

We walked up Wimpole Street together. It is not very far, you told me. You walked hesitantly, watching your feet. You seemed pleased that I was accompanying you. You said very little. After you had taken your key out of your bag, you gave me a small card. Do ring me, you said.

I was awkward on the telephone. I have no ease with the thing. I settled in to listening, and that seemed not to displease either of us. When I said a word at all – and I interjected two or three – you savoured it, I felt. You seemed grateful that I had made the effort. You perhaps understood me a little. You had gone a little further every day, you told me, and today you had walked as far as Regent's Park, which felt like a miracle, you said, because, when you first started out, you had felt so tentative...

The day the Bechstein Room re-opened coincided with a concert of chamber music by Bartok, including the second string quartet. Hallelujah! To my horror, there were no returns. I stood beside the wall, and waited. Sure enough, my luck held. A last-minute cancellation due to illness. I saw you in the auditorium, three rows from the front. You looked round, as if scanning the hall for my presence. We waved at each other. It had all begun again, gently, tentatively, as it would always be between us. After all, we were of a certain age.

After a decent interlude had elapsed, you invited me up

for coffee. Should I accept? I accepted. It was the Dvorak day. Dvorak – I see it now quite clearly, with the benefit of hindsight – came between us. How silly of us to let it! We were talking, as we often did, about music, how it bears meaning, and especially chamber music. You sat on the edge of your chair. You were impassioned as usual. I was in the habit of arguing for the sake of it, to throwing out a proposition or two, just to see where it led you. You were unaccustomed to that sort of thing. You looked gravely serious when I mentioned the second movement of his String Quartet, No. 11 in C, his opus 61. We had just been listening to it. The charm and the overbearing melancholy of chamber music, I said, is that it always looks back, to vanished worlds of human feeling. It is essentially nostalgic. It never urges us to act, merely to reflect, misty-eyed. It throws open the past like a great yawning door. You looked puzzled when I said that. And so I continued. Have you not noticed how no one ever moves? That utter stillness? How one's eyes surf over a sea of motionless grey heads? Bodily impulses are entirely absent.

You got up just then, quite briskly, and walked over to the window. You said nothing. You wrapped your arms about yourself as if you were sickening for something. Are you quite all right? I asked you. Not completely, you replied. And then I left. It seemed the right thing to do.

The streets were so still. I took a left towards Cavendish Square. I felt such a cleansing absence of human life just then. And yet there was nothing else there either, no god on this Sunday morning. There was such an overbearing absence of birds. I could hear that second movement again inside my head, replaying itself. The musicians had been Czech, middle-aged, all male. I heard again how those furious threads of melody were being passed, back and forth, between the first and the second violin. How clear the light seemed just then, boundless the blueness of the sky.

If I were ever to see you again, I was thinking to myself, what exactly would it mean?

REVOLUTIONS

He was moving at walking pace, shuffling steadily forwards, all day and all night, from first to last light. And we were all out there in the street with our mouths gaping open. My god, it seemed like a miracle to us – well, you could call it that if you like, I suppose, but I, for one, well, I wasn't so sure that was the right thing to call it...

How did he do it though? Who had given him back the strength in his legs? I can see them now, those legs of his, thin and brittle as birch twigs you might snap across your knee. Who'd asked him to do all that walking in the first place? It was not as if he'd been well for years...

I used to see him every day, pottering about that pokey kitchen garden of his, not doing anything but walk stiff and slow between his sticks, arms trembling, or maybe taking the odd side swipe at the head of a potato flower, those lovely flowers. Sad really. He didn't have the strength to dig them up after the flowers faded. He couldn't even lean down and pick himself a bunch of those forget-me-nots that were once so dear to him. He loved the blue of them, he said. You could stare deeper into the heart of a tiny forget-me-not than any other flower, he said. He may have been right about that for all I know. I'm not much for flowers myself, but that garden of his was a sea of blue come April, May time.

It was lucky we were there to lend a hand all those years or I reckon he wouldn't have got through it. That doctor lost patience with him, the way he poured all the medicine down the sink. We would hear him shouting at him – and he was normally such a tranquil old soul, Dr Marston, warning him for the very last time to swallow the stuff down as instructed or he'd never get well again, he could promise him that. But did he listen? Did he heck. He just turned his face to the wall and heaved a great long sigh, as if to say: if I lie here long enough not speaking, his shadow will fade from the wall. Oh, he could be that stubborn, Harold Beasley.

Well, of course, he got worse after that, after the doctor washed his hands of him. But we couldn't let him starve. We couldn't just sit back in our chairs and let him fade away now, could we? We had a duty to care for him, a bounden Christian duty. God would be pointing a pretty stern finger at all of us by and by if we let him go to nothing, even if it was cantankerous old Harold Beasley – and none of us could abide him, let me make that quite plain. He didn't have one friend left in the world after queer Cyril died, not one.

So we talked about it, we had meetings, then more meetings, chewing it all over, what in the world we could do to help him, just to keep him alive. Well, there were fourteen of us Chapel people, one for each day of the fortnight, and so that's what we did. Every day one of us would be responsible for calling on him and doing the odd thing or two just to keep him ticking over. That's all he ever wanted from life, I swear to it, just to tick over. He was a lazy old B, even in his prime, that blinkin' Harold Beasley.

And I'll never forget it, the very first time it was my turn to call on him. I freely admit, I didn't want to go. God above knew that – not a bit of it – because he could see into my heart. But I had to, I knew that I had to. So I went. I took myself off down the road with a little bundle of things, nothing much, clutched tight in my hand, and when I came to that door of his, that great heavy barn of a door with the old brown paint flaking off – it was such a sight for sore eyes, that door, he had no pride in himself or his belongings, never had had. God, that place was falling down around his ears even before he started to go bad. There were birds nesting in his thatch, the chimney unswept, and such a heap of old rubbish piled up by the door... Yes, that's what he always did when he'd done with anything, no matter what, just open the door and chuck it out, fish, flesh or skin and bone of fowl, tin can, busted kettle, bent nail, no matter what. Oh, no such refinery as dustbins for the likes of Harold Beasley, no, he didn't believe in such new-fangled things.

So there it was, that great stinking heap that you had to step round before you could even reach for the knocker attached to his door.

Well, I didn't half hammer it down on that wood, but not on purpose or anything, not to alarm him or to make him come running. The last thing on earth that I wanted was to see him there scowling and muttering his oaths, of which he had the ripest collection known to mankind. God alone knows where he got them, perhaps from the mouth of the devil himself.

No, the thing was, the reason I had to swing it so hard, was the stiffness of it. My god, it scarcely moved, no matter how much force you used against it. Still, having loosened it up with a swing or two, it did its job and, by and by, I heard him come shiffly-shuffling along, mumbling and muttering those words to himself.

I could tell he was complaining as usual. He never wanted to be disturbed, that Harold Beasley, no matter if he was up to his neck in filth and misfortune. Did he care? But *we* cared because God cared. God cares for the least of them, yes, even for *that* one he cared – *and* he died. Even for Harold Beasley he died, though it took some imagining when I saw that narrowed eye of his through a chink of the door. And, my God, what a greeting he gave me, poking his stick through the door and jabbing it at my legs as if it was some mangy old stray that had come knocking just for the privilege of snapping at his heels.

'Harold Beasley!' I said – no, I wasn't afraid to give him an earful, oh no, not when my body was threatened so rudely – 'Harold Beasley, put down that stick or I'll snatch it from your hand – and then how will you stand upright on your legs? You'll be reduced to crawling like the rest of the animal kingdom, won't you?'

Well, deaf though he always said he was, he drew it in slowly, grudgingly slowly, and I could hear how the phlegm rattled in his throat as he did it – like thunder receding. Still, I'd got what I wanted. I'd tidied that first bit of mischief away.

And then what does he do – oh, the nerve of it! – but start, quietly, oh so gradually, closing it up again... So I grabs at the end of the stick, the tail end, just before it vanishes from sight altogether, and I pulls and I pulls at it, shouting: 'Hey, I'm here for your own good if you did but know it!' And that scratchy old voice of his shouts back: 'What good are the likes of you to me?' And he starts pulling it back again.

A right little tug of war we had, just the two of us. Nothing wrong with his arms then, I was thinking to myself, though the legs may be close to collapsing. But I did it all right, by pushing and pulling and jiggling and wiggling it, I prised it back far enough, that door, just enough to grab at his bony old hand, so cold and so terribly bony, that was clutching the stick, gripping it fast as a limpet.

'Now show a bit of sense, Harold Beasley,' I said, still wiggling and pushing it back with my knee for good measure. 'Don't you know who it is then that's pulling on the nether end of your stick? Have you seen this face before? Can you pretend that you haven't?'

Well then he stopped, didn't he. And I stopped too. And he looked at me, squinting and scowly-frowning as if I were some termite on two legs come to plague him inside his shirt. Then he let go of the thing, just like that, left me just standing there with it, hanging loose, and the door fell back, and he shuffled off back to the darkness of that God-forsaken kitchen of his where he always would sit, staring, and smoking that stinking black shag of his.

But I followed him in all right. I was meaning to get something done in this place. There was human life squatting here, night and day, life of a sort anyway, that God would never, not in a month of Sundays, disown, so there I went, stamping in behind him, for the Saviour's sake – and his too if he did but know it.

Well, you'd never believe it, I'm sure, but he had not one scrap of food in the place, not a slice of stale bread, not a smidgen of butter, not the tail end of a sardine either. And the sight of the bareness of that cupboard of his when I flung back the doors, and the way those cobwebs were still hanging there loose like the misty drapes of the ghostly dead, well, all that and much more I cannot bear to tell, it just drives me to fury.

'Harold,' I said, turning to face him as he sat slumped down there in his chair like a sackful of turnips, 'Harold, it's a sin what you're doing to yourself, a slap full in the face of the Almighty himself to let yourself go like this.

'How can you hope to stay alive if you don't provide for yourself? What is it that you think you're doing? Committing slow suicide or something? Have you not read that it is the gravest sin in God's book to do that to your body and soul? I'll tell you now so that you'll be forewarned: if you make away with yourself in this dastardly fashion, your body won't get itself decently buried inside those cemetery walls. It's a sin against nature, you know. You'll be thrown on that heap by the door for the carrion to gnaw at you, and the crows to come chuckling down and peck out your eyes...'

Well, I said it, you know, just to scare him a little, knowing full well how superstitious he was. But did he believe it? My God, he did not.

'Out, woman!' he shouts, springing up from that chair,

and waving with fury, those arms going pell mell like the sails of a windmill run mad in the wind. 'I don't want your words, and I don't need the help of you chapel people. I'll live as I please in this house, and I'll die when I'm ready. Out you go!'

But I stood there, firm on my legs, still clutching that bundle, and I said to him, outfacing his ire:

'Harold, there's cheese, high as you like it, and there's three or four goose eggs, the biggest, in this bundle. There's a slice or two of bread too, and I'm leaving it here, and if you don't want it, you can throw it all clean out the window.'

And there I left it, and took my leave.

I tell you the truth, I was fair shaking with anger at the man when I left him. But it was worse for the others, the ones that came after, much worse, so they tell me. That Radcliffe woman, the one with the chin, from the big old house on the corner, she near on lost an eye to that stick of his, the way it came whistling down, swishing and swinging, from the upper window. Oh yes, he was ready for them then, the next time it happened, hanging out the window, cursing and spitting and swinging.

But then, just the day before it was my turn to go up there again, it started, the walking, the walking and walking. He went in a circle, you see, up the village, down back lane, crunching over that gravelly stream bed, the reason his boots were always so wet and so muddied when you saw him, then down to the bridge he went, crossing the fields, and back up the road as far as the monument...

Then up he comes again, always the left hand side of the High Street, never the right. Well, there were a few of them looked when he first went and did it, of course, just to see him out there, on his sticks and, God, what a sight he was, with his hair sticking out, face all red and puffed up with the drinking, and leaning hard on those sticks, half bent over, as he wheezed and he shuffled his way past the house and, every now and then, stopping and blowing out great gouts of breath, chest heaving, like a horse that's ready for the knackers.

Yes, I saw it myself that first time, but I didn't like to see it, if you see what I mean. It pained me, just to see what he was putting himself through, why, in God's name, he needed to do it. But I thought that was the end of it till it happened again – and again – and each time that it happened, the look of him was worse and worse, the pace that much slower and painful. So the fourth time he did it – and now they were lining the street, all those kiddies, shouting things at him, and one of them even took up a stone in her hand, dandled it, threw it...

And then another one, that Kelly child, the consumptive, would you credit it, she starts this chanting at him, beating time on her thin little knees, though she hardly had the breath in herself to say it, but I heard it, they all heard it, and they took it up too, and soon all of them were going at it: scary, scary Scarecrow, beastly, beastly, Beasley, scary, scary, scarecrow... And on and on it went, getting louder and louder and, well, I just couldn't bear it, the beastliness of those children...

So I flung out the door and I shouted out – they were all up there by the wall – shut your mouths or I'll put the lot of you across my knee! And that stopped them straight off. They were all staring back at me, lips trembling, the biggest and the littlest. My, I must have been looking some fierce.

Then I opened the gate and pushed past them to where he was standing, but now he was kneeling, not standing, and one of those sticks of his, they'd taken it from him, the varmints. And when I saw that, I shouted: quick, give me the stick. He's all crippled up, can't you see? He can't walk, he can't move, without the stick. And so back she comes tripping with it, Elly Marston, the doctor's very own fair-haired, beautiful daughter, pride and joy of his life, and she gives it me, prettily balancing it there across my hand without once raising her eyes. But I says to the top of her pretty, bowed head: you ought to be ashamed of your habits, little Elly, you being the doctor's own daughter, and I hear her start blitherin' into her sleeve before she runs back to join all the others, and not one word are they saying, just looking and staring...

But what can I do for him? He's down there, panting, on his hands and his knees, like a dog, and he's trembling like fury, and he can't get his breath, I can see it... So I puts my arm round his shoulders, and I says to him, trying my best not to take in the foul smell of his hair, like the coat of a sow that's been rolling in muck all day: Harold, I says, just you sit up a little, easy now does it, now lean on me, take this stick in your hand, and lift up that knee... well, I'm talking to him in slow, easy words, like a child that needs tutoring, but it's the best thing for him, I know it, because he's moving now, and doing the things I tell him...

And back we go then, through the throng of those children, just the two of us, arms linked together, one stick tapping forward, and me grasping the other, all ready to swipe at the first one that sniggers.

Then we're indoors, through the door of the parlour, and he falls with a groan, flat, on his back, like a sack, on the sofa, and he closes his eyes. And I yank shut the curtains to block off the stares of those nebby old neighbours.

And it's dark in that room, so dark, and so dingy, on account of my mother's best old worsted curtains, and all I can see in that gloom is the rise and the fall of his chest, and all I can hear is the wheeze of his troubled breathing. And I'm squatting there, tense, on the edge of that chair, knees crossed, gnawing my nails, staring at the shape of his body and thinking: Harold Beasley, you are so beastly, oh man, you're so beastly. It's true, all that chanting, every word of it's true. You never once paid any heed to the needs of another. You lived for yourself and you'll die for yourself, lonely, bitter, unwanted.

God, let Him have you just as soon as he likes, and I don't, not one bit of me, care if he hears it, what I'm saying out loud, practically screaming, in the quiet of my mind. Let Him hear it. He's known all along, Christ Jesus, how I've suffered, thirty years how I suffered your insults, your lies and your ravings. He knows – like I know – that you fell at my door for a reason just now. He knows – and you know – why you did it. You wanted me there at the window, to see it, take pity, and, eyes blinded with tears, come running.

You did it that first time I strewed your things over the garden, your trousers, your shirts, and those stringy old braces I hung from the ash tree to mock you. I locked you out too, and you wailed and you bellowed, and you marched round the village, round and round the village, like some poor, benighted, suffering thing, wits all gone astray. And I let you back in – more fool me! – to douse all that fuss and commotion. My God, I wish I hadn't!

And now you're here again, you're lying here again, and I've done it, what I always swore I wouldn't. Oh merciful Christ, lamp of hope, won't you just once tell him to take up his bed and walk right out of my life? I cannot bear these revolutions. But don't please, let him die by his own hand, Lord, because that we could neither forgive nor understand.

Publisher's Note

1889 Books is a practically zero budget undertaking, bringing books to readers for the sheer love of it. It is a small undertaking with no marketing resources, so if you enjoyed reading this it would be great if you could do a quick review on Amazon, Goodreads or whatever book review sites you use: a line or two would be great. Reviews and personal recommendations are really appreciated by authors and small publishers and help us to keep doing what we do. Thanks!